THADY SHEA'S SAGA

H. BEDFORD-JONES

THADY SHEA'S SAGA

H. BEDFORD-JONES

COVER ILLUSTRATION BY

HERBERT MORTON STOOPS

ALTUS PRESS • 2016

PUBLISHING HISTORY

"Thady Shea's Saga" originally appeared in the October, 1919–February 1920 issues of *People's* magazine (Vol. 31, No. 5–Vol. 32, No. 2).

THANKS TO

Gerd Pircher

TABLE OF CONTENTS

CHAPTER I

THE MAN WHO HAD BEEN

A RIBBON OF winding road leads northeast from
the pueblo of Domingo and the snaky Bajada hill where
gray rocks lie thickly; it is a yellowish ribbon of road, sweeping
over the gigantic mesa toward Santa Fé and the sweetly glowing
Blood of Christ peaks—great peaks of green spearing into the
sky, white-crested, and tipped with blood at sunset.

Along this ribbon of dusty yellow road was crawling a flivver.
It was crawling slowly, in a jerky series of advances and pauses;
as it crept along its intermittent course, the woman who sat
behind the wheel was cursing her iron steed in a thorough and
heartfelt manner.

Both in flivver and woman was that which fired curious
interest. The rear of the car was piled high with boxes and
luggage; certain of the boxes were marked "Explosives—Handle
With Care!" Prominent among this freight was a burlap sack
tied about the neck and firmly roped to one of the top supports
of the car.

The woman was garbed in ragged but neat khaki. From
beneath the edges of an old-fashioned bonnet, tied beneath the
chin, protruded wisps of grayish hair, like an aureole of silver.
The woman herself was of strikingly large frame and great in
girth; her arms, bare to the elbows, were huge in size. Yet this
giantess was not unhealthily fat. Hardened by toil, her hands
were gripped carefully upon the steering wheel as though she

were in some fear of wrenching it asunder in an unguarded moment.

Her features were large, sun-darkened, creased and seamed with crow's-feet that betokened long exposure to wind and weather. Ever and anon she drew, with manifest enjoyment, at an old brown corncob pipe. Above her firm lips and beak-like nose a pair of blue eyes struck out gaily and keenly at the world; eyes of a piercing, intense blue, whose brilliancy, as of living jewels, gave the lie to their surrounding tokens of toil and age.

"Drat it!" she burst forth, after a new bucking endeavour on the part of the car. "If I was to shoot this damned thing through the innards, maybe she'd quit sunfishin' on me! I'm goin' to sell her to Santy Fé sure's shooting; I'll get me a pair o' mules and a wagon, then I'll know what I'm doing. Dunno how come I ever was roped into buying this here contraption—"

She suddenly halted her observations. Laying aside her pipe and peering out from the side of the dusty windshield, her keen eyes narrowed upon the road ahead.

Against that yellowish ribbon, with its bordering emptiness of mesquite, greasewood, and sage, there was nothing moving; but squarely in the centre of the road showed up a dark, motionless blotch. It was the figure of a man lying as though asleep. No man would or could lie asleep in the middle of this road, however, under the withering blaze of the downpouring New Mexico sun.

Suddenly the fitful flivver coughed under more gas; it roared, bucked, darted ahead, bucked again, and a dozen yards from the prostrate man it went leaping forward as though impelled by vindictive spite to run over the motionless figure. The woman swore savagely. She seemed inexperienced as a chauffeuse; only by a hair's breadth did she manage to avoid the man, and then she stopped the car.

Her great size became more apparent as she alighted. Standing, she gazed down at the man, then leaned forward and turned

His blazing black eyes stared into the gaze of Ross.

the unfortunate vagrant upon his back. The body was listless to her hand, the head lolled idly.

"Hm!" said the woman, reflectively. "Ain't drunk. Ain't hurt. Hm!"

She reached into the car and produced a whiskey flask, then sat down in the dust and took upon her ample lap the head of the senseless man. A sudden deftness became manifest in her motions, an unguessed tenderness relieved the harshness of her features.

"This here is breakin' the law," she ruminated, pouring liquor between the lips of the vagrant, "but it ain't the first time Mehitabel Crump has broke laws to help some poor devil! Hm! Looks to me like he ain't et for quite a spell."

With increasing interest she surveyed the slowly reviving stranger.

He was fully as lank as she was stout, and must have stood a good six foot two in height. His clothes were tattered remnants of once sober black. Long locks of iron-gray hair hung about his ears. His features were careworn and haggard, yet in them lingered some indefinable suggestion of fine lines and deeply carven strength. Had Mehitabel Crump ever viewed Sir Henry Irving—which she had not—she might have guessed a few things about her "find."

Suddenly the eyes, the intensely black eyes, of the man opened. So did his lips.

"Angels and ministers of grace!" His voice, although faint, was touched with a deep intonation, a roundness of the vowels, a clarity of accent. "As I do live and breathe, it is the kiss of lordly Bacchus which doth welcome me!"

"Take it calm," advised Mehitabel Crump, pityingly. "You'll have your right sense pretty soon. Many's the time I've seen Crump keeled over, and come to with his mind awandering. Jest take it calm, pilgrim. I'll have a bite o' cornbread—"

She lowered his head to the dust, rose, and went to the flivver. Presently she returned with a slab of cold cornbread divided by bacon, and a desert water bottle.

"Heaps o' lunch in the car." She aided the gaunt one to sit up, and he clutched at the food feverishly. "My land! Ain't et real frequent lately, have ye?"

The man, his mouth full, shook his head dumbly. About his eyes was a brilliancy which told of sheer starvation. To the full as worldly wise as any person in broad New Mexico, the woman asked no questions as yet; she procured from the car a basket which contained the remainder of her luncheon, and set forth the contents.

"Figgered I might get held up 'fore reaching Santy Fé. If it warn't that dratted car, it sure would be something else, which same it is. Damned good luck it ain't worse, as Crump used to say when Providence went agin' him."

She observed that the stranger ate ravenously, but drank sparingly. Not thirst had downed him, but starvation.

He seemed startled at her disconcertingly frank manner of speech. She put him down as something better than an ordinary hobo; an out-of-luck Easterner, possibly a lunger. He was fifty or so; with decent clothes, a shave, and a haircut, he might be a striking-looking fellow, she decided. Although he had a hard mouth, what Mehitabel Crump had learned to know as a whiskey mouth, it was steady lipped.

"You sure played in tough luck comin' this road," she said, musingly. "So did I. Ain't nothing between here and Santy Fé 'cept Injuns, greasers, and rattlers, any one of which is worse'n the other two. These rocks is playin' hell with my tires and the old Henry is coughin' fit to bust her innards. If I find the feller who sold her to me, I'd sure lay him one over the ear!"

Her simple meal finished, she began to stuff her corncob pipe. The man, still eating wolfishly, watched her with fascinated eyes. She gazed out at the snowy, sun-flooded Sangre de Cristo peaks and continued her soliloquy. When it suited her, Mehitabel Crump could be very garrulous; and when it suited her, she could be as taciturn as the mountains themselves.

"I ain't surprised at nothing no more, not these days. No, sir! When I first come to this country you knowed just what ye had to reckon agin'. They was Injuns to fight, greasers to work devilment, claim jumpers to rob ye, and such. But now the Injuns is all towerist peddlers, the greasers is called 'natives' and runs the courts an' legislature, and gun toting ain't popular. A lone woman gets skinned plumb legal, when in the old days it would ha' been suicide to rob a female. Yes pilgrim, set right in at what's left, and don't bother to talk yet a spell."

She touched a match to her pipe, broke the match, tossed it away.

"If Crump hadn't blowed up with a dry fuse in a shaft we was sinking over in the Mogollons, where we was prospecting at the time, he'd be plumb astonished at the changes. Yes, and I bet he'd swear to see me driving one of them contraptions yonder! Poor Crump, I never had the heart to dig him up, though it was a right smart prospect we was workin'. But somehow I couldn't never work that claim, with him still in it that-a-way. I won't need the money, neither, if I've got hold of—"

She paused. Her gaze went to the devouring stranger. Abruptly she changed the subject.

"You don't look like you was much more'n a poor, innercent pilgrim without any brains to mention. Yet, stranger, I'd gamble that we'd stack up high in morals agin' such old-timers as Abel Dorales, him what's half greaser and half Mormon, or old Sandy Mackintavers, what come straight from Scotland to Arizony and made a forchin in thirty years of thieving! Yes, I reckon ye've got a streak of real pay dirt in ye, stranger. And if I can't tell what breed o' cattle a man is by jest looking at him, it's a queer thing! I've knowed 'em all."

The complimented pilgrim bolted the last scrap of food in sight, raised the canvas bag to his lips, and drank. Sighing, he wiped his lips with the frayed cuff of his sleeve. Then he disentangled his long legs and rose. One hand upon his heart, the other flourished magnificently, he made a bow that was the piteous ghost of a perished grandeur.

"Madam!" His voice rang out firmly now, a deep and sonorous bass. "Madam, I thank you! In me you behold one who has received the plaudits of thousands, one who has bowed to the thunderous acclaim of—"

"What d'ye say your name was?" snapped Mehitabel Crump. Her voice was suddenly acid, her blue eyes ice. The other was manifestly disconcerted by her change of front.

"Madam, I am familiarly known as Thaddeus Roscius Shea. Under the more imposing title of Montalembert I have made known to thousands the aspiring genius of the immortal Avonian bard. I avow it, madam—I am a Thespian! I suit the action to the word, the word to the action—"

"Huh!" cut in his audience with a ruthless lack of awe. "Huh! Never heard of them Thespians, but likely it's a new Mormon sect. I knowed a man of your name down to Silver City twelve year back; this Thady Shea was a good fightin' man, with one eye and a harelip. Glad to meet ye, pilgrim! I'm Mehitabel Crump, with Mrs. for a handle."

Something in her manner seemed mightily to embarrass Mr. Shea, but he took a fresh start and set forth to conquer the difficulty.

"Madam, a Thespian is of no religious persuasion, but one who treads the boards and who wears the buskin of Thespis. You behold in me the first tragedian of the age. My *Hamlet,* madam, has been praised by discerning critics from Medicine Hat to Jersey City. The accursed moving pictures have ruined my art."

"Oh! It's usually whiskey or woman," said Mrs. Crump, her eyes ominous. "So you're a stage actor, eh? Then that explains it."

"Explains, madam? Explains what?" faltered Shea, sensing a gathering storm.

"Your damn foolishness. Shake it off, ye poor hobo! I no sooner hands ye a bit o' kindness than it swells ye up like a balloon. Now, don't you get gay with *me,* savvy? Don't come none o' that high-falutin' talk with me, or by hell I'll paralyze ye! I did think for a minute that ye had the makin's of a man, but I apologize."

The blue eyes turned away. Had Shea been able to see them, he might have read in them a look that did not correspond to Mrs. Crump's spoken word. But he did not see them.

He turned away from the woman. The carven lines of his face deepened, aged, as from him was rent the veil of his posturing. A weary and hopeless sadness welled in his eyes; the sadness of one who beholds around him the wreckage of all his little world, brought down to ruin by his own faults. When he spoke, it was with the same sonorous voice, yet lacking the fine rolling accent.

"You are right, Mrs. Crump, you are right. God help me! I, who was once a man, am now less than the very dust. Your harshness is justified. At this time yesterday, madam, I was a wretched drunken fool, spouting lines of rhetoric in Albuquerque."

"I'm surprised at that," said Mrs. Crump. "How'd ye get the liquor, since this here state an' nation ain't particularly wet no more? And how ye got here from Albuquerque I don't figger."

"It is simply told." From the miserable Shea was stripped the last vestige of his punctured pose. "Twenty years ago my young wife died, and I started upon the whiskey trail; it has led me— here. Yesterday I came into Albuquerque, starving. At the railroad station, amid some—er—confusion, I encountered a company of those motion picture men who dare to call themselves actors. So far was my pride broken that I begged of them help in the name and memory of The Profession."

Shea emphatically capitalized these last two words.

"They took me aboard their train," he pursued, "and I was given drink. Some controversy arose, I know not how; I found myself ignominiously ejected from the train. I walked, not knowing nor caring whither. Nor is that all, madam. I am a fugitive from justice!"

"Broke jail?" queried Mrs. Crump, betraying signs of interest.

"No, madam. In Albuquerque I was starving and desperate. I—I stole fruit and—sandwiches—from a railroad stand."

His voice failed. He turned away, staring at the snowy peaks as though awaiting a verdict.

"Pretty low-down and worthless, ain't ye?" Mrs. Crump checked herself suddenly, glancing at the yellow ribbon of road over which she had so recently come. A flying cloud of dust gave notice of the approach of a large automobile.

Suddenly rising, Mrs. Crump knocked out her pipe, then caught Shea by the shoulder. Her hand swung him about as though he were a child. His eyes widened in surprise upon meeting the warm regard in her face, the steady and sympathetic smile upon her lips.

"Thady," she said, bluntly, "how old are ye?"

"Fifty-eight," he mumbled in astonishment.

"Huh! Two year older'n me. Made a mess of your life, ain't ye? Don't know as I blame ye none, Thady. When Crump passed out, I come near throwin' up the sponge; but I got to fightin' and I been fightin' ever since, and here I am! Now, Thady, you got strength and you got guts; I can see it in your eye. All ye need is backbone. Why don't ye buck up?"

"I've tried," he faltered, controlled by her personality. "It's no use—"

"You go get in that car." Mrs. Crump glanced again at the approaching automobile, then half flung the gaunt Shea toward her dust-white flivver. "Get in and don't say a word, savvy? One thing about you, ye can be trusted—which is more'n can be said for some skunks in this here country! Get in, now, and leave me palaver with Sheriff Tracy."

Shea, shivering at mention of the sheriff, jack-knifed his length upon the car's front seat.

From some mysterious recess of her ample person Mrs. Crump produced an immense old-fashioned revolver, which she began to burnish with seeming absorption. The big automobile slowed up. It halted a few feet behind the flivver, and a hearty hail came forth.

"By jingoes, if it ain't Mis' Crump! Hello, old-timer—ain't seen you in ages!"

From the car sprang a hale and vigorous man who advanced with hand extended.

"I kind o' thought it was you, Sam Tracy," said Mrs. Crump. "Thought I recognized that there car o' yours. How's the folks?"

"All fine. And you? But I needn't ask—why, you grow younger every month—"

"See here! What ye doin' over in this county, Sam? Why don't ye get back to Bernalillo where ye belong?"

The sheriff waved his hand.

"Going to Santy Fé. I'm looking up a fellow who came this way from Albuquerque—a hobo and sneak thief name o' Shea. Where ye been keepin' yourself, ma'am? It don't seem like the same old state not to see ye from time to time."

"Sam Tracy," observed Mrs. Crump with a look of severity, "I've knowed you more years than I care to reckon up. And you know me, I guess! Now, Sam, I sure hate to do it—but I got to. Stick up your hands, Sam, and do it damn sudden!"

The muzzle of her revolver poked the astounded sheriff in the stomach. For a moment he gazed into her shrewd blue eyes, then slowly elevated his hands.

"Are you crazy, ma'am?" he demanded.

She removed his holstered weapon, then lowered her own and shook her head.

"Nope. I'm heap sane right here and now. Set down and smoke whilst I explain."

CHAPTER II

THADY SHEA
ENCOUNTERS PURPOSE

"**Y**OUR MAN Shea is settin' in my car yonder," said Mrs. Crump.

Heedless of the glaring sun, she picked up her pipe and disposed her giant frame for converse. From narrowed lids the sheriff eyed the lanky, up-drawn figure of Shea, which he now noticed for the first time. Then he produced the "makings" and proceeded to roll a cigarette.

"Glad you picked him up," said he. "I'll take him back with me."

"No, ye won't," retorted Mrs. Crump, calmly. "You'll not touch him, Sam Tracy."

"He's a thief and a drunkard and a hobo," said the sheriff.

"If they wasn't no drinks to be had in heaven, I reckon hell would be majority choice," quoth the lady. "When it comes to that, I've seen you and Crump so paralyzed you couldn't talk. There was that night down to Magdalena when the railroad spur was finished and they held a celebration—"

The sheriff grinned. "No need to argue further along them lines, ma'am. You win!"

"I reckon I do, Sam. Besides, you ain't got no authority over in this county. You can run a bluff on ignorant hoboes an' greasers, but not on Mehitabel Crump! Your authority quit quite a ways back. Thady Shea only stole because he was starving, which I'd do the same in his place. I picked him up here and I'm goin' to keep him."

"You always was soft-hearted," reflected Tracy. "Now you got him, what's your programme?"

Mrs. Crump refilled and lighted her corncob with deliberation, then made response:

"Sam, I'm sure in a thunderin' bad pinch. Damned good luck it ain't worse, as Crump used to say at times. You know I ain't no legal shark, huh? Well, three weeks ago I had a blamed good hole in the hills, until Abel Dorales come along and located just below me. Then in rides old Sandy Mackintavers and offers a thousand even for my hole, saying that Abel had located the thrown apex of my claim—"

"The apex law don't obtain here," put in Tracy.

"I know it; but who's goin' to argue with Mackintavers? If it wasn't that, it'd be somethin' worse. Anyhow, he offered to compromise and so on."

The sheriff nodded. "I see how you come to have the flivver," he observed, drily.

"Yas, ye do!" Mrs. Crump's response was raw-edged. "If you was the kind o' man you used to be, ye'd up and give them jumpers a hemp necktie! But now ye play politics, Sam Tracy, and ye lick the boots o' Sandy Mackintavers—"

"That's enough, Mis' Crump!" broke in the sheriff, icily. "I don't blame ye for feelin' sore, but the likes of us can't fight Mackintavers in the courts. We ain't slick enough! And Dorales is a Mormon-bred greaser, than which the devil ain't never fathered a worse combination. Now, Mis' Crump, you show me the least excuse for doin' it legally, and I'll pump them two men full o' lead any day! I'm only surprised that you didn't do it."

"I did." A smile of grim satisfaction wreathed the lady's firm lips. "First I took Sandy's money, then I lets fly. They was several hired greasers with Dorales, and I reckon I got two-three; ain't right sure. I only got Abel glancingly, and when I threw down on Sandy his arms was both elevated for safety. All I could decently do was to nick his ear so's he'd remember me."

"You didn't kill Dorales?"

"Afraid not." Mrs. Crump sadly shook her head. "I didn't wait to inquire none, but it looked like I'd only blooded his shoulder and he was layin' low to plug me in the back, so I belted him over the head with the butt, and slid for home."

The sheriff, astounded, emitted a long whistle. "Whew-w!" he said, slowly. "Say, whereabouts did all this happen?"

"Down the Mogollons. Over Arizony way."

"Why didn't ye go west into Arizony, then? After that doin's this state will be too hot to hold ye—"

"Oh, Sandy won't go to law over the shootin'. It'd make him look too ridic'lous."

The sheriff threw back his head and laughed with all the uproarious abandon of a man who laughs seldom but well.

"Best look out for yourself," he cautioned. "That there Dorales will be on your trail till hell freezes over, ma'am! I sure would admire to see you in action on that crowd!"

"You'll see me in action when that there car gets movin' again," she retorted. "She bucks like a range hoss and kicks to beat hell—why, I couldn't hardly keep the saddle!"

The sheriff arose and went to the dust-white flivver. He adjusted the spark, cranked, and for a moment listened to the engine before killing it. Then he threw back the hood, and, under the sombre eyes of Thady Shea, worked in silence. At length he finished his task, started the engine again, and with a nod of satisfaction shut it off.

"Thought mebbe so," he stated, rejoining the lady. "Your spark plugs was fouled. Well, ma'am, what can I be doin' for you?"

"Ye might send me a wire in care of Coravel Tio whenever ye get a line on Dorales or Mackintavers. I'm fixing to meet them again."

"How come?" demanded the sheriff in surprise.

Mrs. Crump gestured with her pipe toward the flivver.

"I got a sack of ore in there that I found in the lava beds or thereabouts. I suspicions it's one o' these new-fangled things nobody give a whoop for in the old days, but that draws down the money now. If it is, then you can lay that Sandy will hear I've found it, and he'll be after me to jump the claim."

"He sure does keep a line on prospectors," reflected the sheriff. "And skins 'em, too, mostly. But he does it legal."

"Yep. If this here stuff is any good, Sam, they's going to be some smoke 'fore he gets his paws on it! Where you goin' from here? Back to Albuquerque?"

"Nope. I got some business up at the capital."

"Will ye tote that ore sack and a letter up to Coravel Tio for me—and do it strictly under your hat?"

"You bet I will, ma'am!"

Mrs. Crump unstrapped the burlap sack. With the sheriff's pencil and paper she settled down to write a letter. The process was obviously painful and laborious, but at length it was finished. The sheriff shook hands, picked up the sack, and turned to his car. Mrs Crump had already restored him his revolver.

"Take good care of yourself, ma'am—and your hobo! Adios."

Mrs. Crump watched the trail of dust disappear in the direction of Santa Fé, then she turned to the flivver and looked up at Thady Shea.

"They's a new corncob laying in back somewheres. You can have it, Thady. Get out here and settle down for a spell o' talk. If ye act real good I'll give ye a drink."

"I don't want any," came Shea's muffled voice as he leaned back in search of the pipe.

"That's a lie. You're fair shaking for liquor and a drop will brace ye up."

Shea procured the pipe, filled and lighted, and promptly assumed, as a garment, his usual histrionic pose. The gulp of liquor which Mrs. Crump carefully measured out sent a thin thread of colour into his gaunt, unshaven cheeks.

"Madam, I owe you all," he announced sonorously. "I have not missed the heart of things set forth in this your discourse to the sheriff's ear, and I have gathered that your need is great for the strong arms of friends, the counsel wise—"

"You got it," cut in Mrs. Crump, curtly. "The p'int is, Thady, where do you come in? Listen here, now! I got a good eye for men; ye ain't much account as ye stand, but ye got the makin's. Now cut out the booze and I'll take ye for partner, savvy? What's more, I'll spend a couple o' weeks attending to it that ye *do* cut out the booze! I sure need a partner who ain't liable to sell me out to them heathen. Can ye down the booze, or not?"

Something in her tone cut through the man's posturing like a knife. As a matter of fact, he was miserable in spirit; his soul quivered nakedly before him, and he was ashamed. For a space he did not answer, but stared at the far mountains. The strong tragedy of his face was accentuated and deepened into utter bitterness.

What Mrs. Crump had only vaguely and darkly seen Thady Shea observed clearly and with wonder; yet, just as she missed the more mystical side of it, he missed the more practical side. More diverse creatures wearing human semblance could scarce have been found than these twain, here met upon a desert upland of New Mexico—the woman, a self-reliant mountaineer and prospector who knew only her own little world, the man a drunkard, a broken-down "hamfatter," who knew all the outside world which had rejected him. They had come together from different spheres.

As he sat there staring, he mentally and for the last time reviewed the life that lay behind him; before him uprose all the contemptuous years, the sad wreckage of high hopes and tinsel glories, the hard and wretched fact of liquor. He would shut it out of his mind forever, after to-day, he thought. He would live in the present only, from day to day. He would try a new life— and let the dead bury their dead!

He turned to Mrs. Crump, his sad and earnest eyes looking oddly cynical.

"I do not think it humanly possible that I can resist liquor," he said, gravely. "I am frank with you. It were easy to swear that I would pluck out drowned honour by the roots—but, madam, I think that this morning I am weary of swearing. I have tried to abstain, and I cannot. Always it is the first week or two of torture that downs me—

"You're showin' sense, now," said the lady. "Want to try it or not?"

He rose in the car and attempted a bow in his showy and pitiful manner. In this bow, however, was an element of grace, the more pronounced by its sharp contrast to his gaunt, sombre aspect.

"Madam, I am deeply sensible of the compliment you pay me. Yet, in picking from the gutter a drunken failure, are you wise? I am entirely ignorant of prospecting and—"

"Don't worry none. Ye'll learn that quick enough."

Again Thaddeus bowed. "But, madam, I understand that prospectors go off into the desert places and live. In justice to yourself, do you not think that your enemies might seize viciously upon the least excuse for misinterpretation of character—"

For the first time Shea saw Mehitabel Crump gripped in anger. He paused, aghast.

Her gigantic form quivered with rage then stiffened into towering wrath. Her tanned, age-touched features suddenly hardened into sentient bronze from which her blue eyes blazed forth terribly, jewelled indices of an indomitable and quick-flaming spirit within.

"Thady Shea, it's well for you them words come from an honest heart," said she, with a slow and grim emphasis. "They ain't no one goin' to say a word agin' me, except them for what I don't give a tinker's dam; and if one o' them dasts to say it in my hearin', chain lightnin' is goin' to strike quick and sudden! This here territory—state, I mean—knows Mehitabel Crump and has knowed her for some years back. Paste that in your hat, Thady Shea!"

As some dread lioness hears in dreams the horns and shouts of hunters, and starting erect with bristling front mutters her low and terrible growl of challenge, so Mehitabel Crump defiantly faced Thaddeus.

He, poor soul, inwardly cursed his too-nimble tongue, and shrank visibly from the spectacle of wrath. Before the hurt and amazed eyes of him Mrs. Crump suddenly abandoned her righteous attitude. Having palpably overawed him, she now felt ashamed of herself.

"There, buck up," she brusquely ordered.

"Tell me, now! If I answer for it that ye stay sober a couple o' weeks or so, will ye make the fight?"

"Yes." Hope fought against despair in Shea's voice; he knew his own weakness well.

"All right. Let's go, then!"

"We're going to Santa Fé?"

Mrs. Crump advanced to the front of the flivver, and seized the crank. Then she paused, her blue eyes striking up over the radiator at Shea.

"No, I ain't goin' to Santy Fé; neither are you! We're goin' to the most man-forsaken spot they is in all the world, I reckon. We got grub, and everything else can wait a couple o' weeks or so. Accordin' to the Good Book, Providence was mighty rushed about creation, but I ain't in no special hurry about makin' a man of you—"

Her words were drowned in the engine's roar. Thaddeus Roscius Shea made himself as small as possible; Mrs. Crump crowded in under the wheel, the car swaying to her weight, and they leaped forward.

In silence she drove, pushing the flivver with a speed and abandon which left Shea clinging desperately to his seat. Twenty minutes later an intersecting road made its appearance; Mrs. Crump left the highway and followed this road due north for a couple of miles. There, coming to an east-and-west road which was decidedly rough, she headed west.

"This here's the trail to Cochiti pueblo," she announced, enigmatically.

Four miles of this, and she struck an even worse road that headed northwest. Shea's eyes opened as they progressed. Never in all his life had he encountered such grotesque country as this which now lay on every hand as though evoked by magic—utter desolation of huge rock masses, blistered and calcined by ancient fires, eroded into strange spires and pinnacles of weird formation. To the north towered Dome Rock with its adjacent crater. No sign of life was anywhere in evidence.

Shea was helplessly gripped by the personality of the woman beside him. Mentally he was overborne and awed; physically he was sick—not ill, but downright sick, possibly due to the sparse gulps of liquor which he had downed, possibly to the glaring sun. He cared not whether he lived or died. He felt that this day had brought him to the end of his rope, and that nothing more could matter.

"Getting into the lava beds," observed Mrs. Crump, cheerfully. Shea understood her words only dimly. "This here Henry sure does go pokin' where you'd think nothin' short of a mule could live! The trail peters out a bit farther, then we got to hoof it over to the Rio Grande and make camp."

Poor Shea shivered. The frightful desolation of the scene horrified him. He had never been an outdoor man. His had ever been the weakness, the dependency of the sheltered and civilized being. Contact with this strangely primitive woman frightened him. He felt like babbling in his terror, begging to be taken back and allowed to resume his place among the swine. Here was something new, awful, incredible! But he held his peace.

Had he been able to look a few miles ahead; had he foreseen what lay before him in that camp in White Rock Cañon, a place which in grandeur and inaccessibility rivalled the great cañon of the Colorado; had he known that he was about to tread a trail which few white men had ever followed—in short, had he understood what Mehitabel Crump's plan held in store for him, he would at that moment have yielded up the ghost, cheerfully!

At last, reaching a sheer incline where boulders larger than the car itself filled all the trail and rendered further progress impossible, Mrs. Crump killed her engine and set her brakes hard.

"I guess Henry can lay here all his life and never be stole," she said, with a sigh of relaxation. "Well, Thady, here we are! D'you know what? It ain't lack of ambition that makes folks mis'able and unsatisfied; it's lack o' purpose. Now, I aim to teach ye some purpose, Thady. Look at me! I been prospectin' all my life, and still goin' strong, just because I got a definite object ahead—to strike it rich somewheres!

"Well, climb down. We got to rig up some grub into packs, hoof it to the nearest canoncito, and reach the Rio Grande. It's less'n two mile in a straight line to water, but twenty 'fore we gets there, if we gets there a-tall. Come on, limber up!"

Thaddeus Roscius Shea groaned inaudibly—but limbered up.

CHAPTER III

CORAVEL TIO ENJOYS
A BUSY MORNING

CORAVEL TIO sold curios in the old town of Santa Fé. He also sold antiques, real and fraudulent; he had a wholesale business in Indian wares that extended over the whole land.

Coravel Tio was one of the few Americans who could trace their ancestry in an unbroken line for three hundred years. It was almost exactly three hundred years since the ancestor of Coravel Tio had come to Santa Fé as a conquistador. Coravel Tio was wont to boast of this, an easily proven fact; and, boasting, he had sold the conquistador's battered old armour at least fifty times.

When the boasts of Coravel Tio were questioned, he would admit with a chuckle that he was a philosopher; and do not all philosophers live by lying, señor? There was great truth in him when he was not selling his ancestor's armour to tourists—and even then, if he happened to like the looks of the tourist, he would gently insinuate that as a business man he sold fraudulent wares and lied nobly about them, but that in private he was a philosopher. And the tourists, liking this quaintly naïve speech, bought the more.

It was a big, dark, quiet shop, full of Indian goods and weapons, antique furniture that would have made Chippendale's eyes water, ivories, old paintings, manuscripts from ancient missions. A good half of Coravel Tio's shop was not for sale at any price. Neither, said men, was Coravel Tio.

He was a soft-spoken little man, quiet, of strange smiles and strange silences. His was the art of making silence into a reproof, an assent, a curse. The world of Santa Fé moved about Uncle Coravel and heeded him not, shouldered him aside; and Coravel Tio, knowing his fathers to have been conquistadores, smiled gently at the world. His name was usually dismissed with a shrug—in effect, a huge tribute to him. Talleyrand would have given his soul to have been accorded such treatment from the diplomats of Europe; it would have rendered him invincible.

One of those rare men was Coravel Tio whose faculties, masked by childish gentleness, grow more terribly keen with every passing year. His brain was like a seething volcano—a volcano which seems to be extinct and cold and impotent, yet which holds unguessed fires somewhere deep within itself.

Upon a day, some time following the meeting of Mehitabel Crump with Thady Shea, this Coravel Tio was standing in talk with one Cota, a native member of the legislature then in session.

"But, señor!" was volubly protesting the legislator, with excitement. "They say the majority is assured, that the bill already drawn, that the capital is to be moved to Albuquerque at this very session!"

"I know," said Coravel, passively, his dark eyes gently mournful.

"You know? But what—what is to be done? Shall those down-state people take away our capital? We must prevent it! We must do something! It's this man Mackintavers who is at the bottom of it, I suppose—"

Coravel Tio fingered a blanket which topped a pile beside him—a gaudy red blanket. He regarded it with curious eyes.

"I fear this is not genuine—it does not have the old Spanish uniform red," he murmured, as though inwardly he were thinking only of his wares. Then suddenly his eyes lifted to the other man, and he smiled. In his smile was a piercing hint of mockery like a half-sheathed sword; before that smile Cota stammered and fell silent.

"Oh, señor, this matter of the capital!" answered Coravel Tio, softly. "Why, for many, many years men have said that the capital is to be moved to Albuquerque; yet it has not been moved! Nor will it be moved. And, Señor Cota, let me whisper something to you! I hear that you have bought a new automobile. That is very nice, very nice! But, señor, if by any chance you are misled into voting for that bill, it would be a very sad event in your life; a most unhappy event, I assure you! Señor, customers await me. *Adios.*"

As the legislator left the shop, he furtively crossed himself, wonder and fear struggling in his pallid features.

The merchant now turned to his waiting customers. Of these, one was a Pueblo, a Cochiti man as the fashion of his high white moccasins and barbaric apparel testified to a knowing eye. The others were two white men who together approached the curio dealer. Coravel Tio stepped to a show case filled with onyx and other old carvings, and across this faced the two men with an uplift of his brows, a silent questioning.

"You're Mr. Coravel—Coravel Tio?" queried one of the two. The dealer merely smiled and nodded, in his birdlike fashion. "Can we see you in private?"

"I have no privacy," said Coravel Tio. "This is my shop. You may speak freely."

"Huh!" grunted the other, surveying him in obvious hesitation. "Well, I dunno. Me and my partner here have been workin' down to Magdalena, and we had a scrap with some fellers and laid 'em out. Right after that, a native by the name of Baca tipped us off that they was Mackintavers' men, and we'd better light out in a hurry. He give us a loan and said to tell you about it, so we lit out here."

Coravel Tio seemed greatly puzzled by this tale.

"My dear sir," he returned, slowly, "I am a curio dealer. I do not know why you were sent to me. Do you?"

"Hell, no!" The miner stared at him disgustedly. "Must ha' been some mistake."

"Undoubtedly. I am most sorry. However, if you are looking for work, I might be able to help you—it seems to me that someone wrote me for a couple of men. Excuse me one moment while I look up the letter. What are your names, my friends?"

"Me? I'm Joe Gilbert. My partner here is Alf Lewis."

Coravel Tio left them, and crossed to a glassed-in box of an office. He opened a locked safe, swiftly inspected a telegraph form, and nodded to himself in a satisfied manner. He returned to the two men, tapped for a moment upon the glass counter, meditatively, then addressed them.

"Señors, I regret the mistake exceedingly. Still, if you want work, I suggest that you drive over to Domingo this afternoon with my cousin, who lives there. You may stay a day or two with him, then this friend of mine will pick you up and take you to work."

The second man, Lewis, spoke up hesitantly.

"Minin' is our work, mister. We ain't no ranchers."

"Certainly." Coravel Tio smiled, gazing at him. "You will not work for a native, my friends. Ah, no! Be here at two this afternoon, please."

The two men left the shop. Outside, in the Street, they paused and looked at each other. The second man, Lewis, swore under his breath.

"Joe, how in hell did he know we was worried over workin' for a greaser boss?"

Gilbert merely shrugged his shoulders and strode away.

Within the shop, Coravel Tio turned to the waiting Indian and spoke—this time neither in Spanish nor English, but in the Indian tongue itself. As he spoke, however, he saw the stolid redskin make a slight gesture. Catlike, Coravel Tio turned about and went to meet a man who had just entered the shop; catlike, too, he purred suave greeting.

A large man, this new arrival—square of head and jaw and shoulder, with small gray eyes closely set, a moustache bristling over a square mouth, ruthless hardness stamped in every line of figure, face, and manner. He was dressed carelessly but well.

"Morning," he said, curtly. His eyes bit sharply about the place, then rested with intent scrutiny upon the proprietor. "Morning, Coravel Tio. I been looking for someone who can talk Injun. I've got a proposition that won't handle well in Spanish; it's got to be put to 'em in their own tongue. I hear that you can find me someone."

Regretfully, Coravel Tio shook his head.

"No—o," he said, in reflective accents. "I am sorry, Mr. Mackintavers. My clerk, Juan Estrada, spoke their language, but he joined the army and is still in service. Myself, I know of it only a word or two. But wait! Here is a Cochiti man who sells me turquoise; he might serve you as interpreter, if he is willing."

He called the loitering Indian, and in the bastard Spanish patois of the country put the query. Mackintavers, who also spoke the tongue well, intervened and tried to employ the Indian as interpreter. To both interrogators the Pueblo shook his head in stolid negation. He would not serve in the desired capacity, and knew of no one else who would.

"It is a great pity he is so stubborn!" Coravel Tio gestured in despair as he turned to his visitor. "I owe you thanks, Mr. Mackintavers, for getting my wholesale department that order from the St. Louis dealer. I am in your debt, and I shall be grateful if I can repay the obligation. In this case, alas, I am powerless!"

"Well, let it go." Mackintavers waved a large, square hand. He produced cigars, set one between his square white teeth, and handed the other to Coravel Tio. "You can repay me here and now. A man at Albuquerque sent a telegram to that Crump woman in your care. Where is she?"

"What is all this?" Coravel Tio was obviously astonished. "Señor, I am a curio dealer, no more! You surely do not refer to the kind-hearted Mrs. Crump?"

Mackintavers eyed him, chewing on his cigar. Then he nodded grimly.

"I do! Is she a particular friend of yours?"

"Certainly! Have I not known her these twenty years? I buy much from her—bits of turquoise, queer Indian things, odd relics. Her mail often comes here, remaining until she calls for it. I am a curio dealer, señor, and in other matters I take no interest."

"Hm!" grunted Mackintavers. "Has she been here lately?"

"No, señor, not for three months—no, more than that! Mail comes, also telegrams."

"D'you know where she is?" demanded the other, savagely.

Dreamily reflective, Coravel Tio fastened his eyes upon the right ear of Mackintavers. That ear bore a half-healed scar, like a bullet-nick. Beneath that silent scrutiny the other man reddened uneasily.

"Let me see! My wife's second cousin, Estevan Baca, wrote me last week that he had met her in Las Vegas. Everyone knows her, señor. If I can send any message for you—"

"No. Much obliged, all the same," grunted the other. "I'll probably be at the Aztec House for a few days. Let me know in case she comes to town, will you? I want to see her."

With exactly the proper degree of bland eagerness, Coravel Tio assented to this, and Mackintavers departed heavily. The merchant accompanied him to the door and watched him stride up the narrow street, cursing the burros laden with mountain wood that blocked his way. Then, smiling a trifle oddly, the descendant of conquistadores returned to the waiting man from Cochiti pueblo.

"Do you know why that man wanted an interpreter?" he asked the Indian, in the latter's native tongue. The redskin grinned wisely and shook the black hair from his eyes.

"Yes. But it is not a matter to discuss with Christians, my father."

Coravel Tio nodded carelessly. The question was closed. The Pueblo folk are, of course, very devoted converts to the Christian faith; yet those who know them intimately can testify that they sometimes have affairs, perhaps touching upon the queer stone idols of their fathers, which do not bear discussion with other Christians. They do not pray to the old gods—perhaps—but they hold them in tremendous respect.

"You came to tell me something," prompted the curio dealer, gently.

The Indian assented with a nod. He leaned against one of the wooden pillars that supported the roof, and began to roll a cigarette while he talked.

"Yesterday, my father, I was near the painted caves of the Colorado, and I stood above White Rock Cañon looking down at the river. There on the other side of the water I saw the strangest thing in the world. I went home and told the governor of the pueblo what I had seen, and it was his command that I come here and tell you also, for this is some queer affair of the white people."

Coravel Tio said nothing at all. The Pueblo lighted his cigarette and continued:

"Upon the east side of the river and cañon, not so well hidden that I could not see it, was a camp, and in that camp were a white man and a white woman. I have never before seen white folk able to reach that place, unless it were the Trail Runner who takes pictures of us and sells them to tourists. These were strangers to me. One was a very large woman. The man was tall, but he acted very strangely. He acted as though God had touched his brain. So did they both."

"In what way?" asked Coravel Tio, sharply.

"In every way, my father. The man wore no shoes, and the hot rocks hurt his feet so that he limped. I saw him spring on the woman, and they fought. She beat him off and pointed a gun at him. Then he seemed to be weeping like a woman, and he grovelled before her. She threw something far off on the stones, and I think it was glass that broke—a bottle, perhaps."

"Oh!" said Coravel Tio. "Oh! Perhaps it was."

"There were other strange actions," pursued the stolid red man. "I could not understand them—"

"No matter." Coravel Tio made a gesture as though dismissing the subject. "Could you get to that camp from your pueblo?"

"Of course, by crossing the river, by swimming the water there. But that may be a hard thing to do, my father."

"Undoubtedly, but you will do it, and I will pay you well. There is a package to give that woman. Wait."

Coravel Tio went to his little box of an office, seated himself at the desk, and began to write in a fair, round hand. The epistle required neither superscription nor signature:

The burlap sack proved to contain some interesting contents. The two small sacks in the centre were even more interesting. The samples have been assayed with the following results:

Numbers one to five, quartzitic with bare traces of brittle silver ore; no good. Numbers six to fifteen, barytes, perhaps five dollars a ton; no good. Number sixteen is strontianite. This is converted into certain nitrates used in manufacture of fireworks and in beet sugar refining. Tremendously valuable and rare. This, señora, is enough.

I think that M. has scented those assays. He is asking for you, but I have made him look toward Las Vegas. To-morrow you will find two men at Domingo who wish work—they will be there until you arrive: Joe Gilbert and Alf Lewis. Meet me there also, please. I will take one-third interest in Number Sixteen as you suggest, and will furnish whatever money you desire on account. I enclose an advance sum.

I shall have articles of partnership ready. Suppose you meet me day after to-morrow, at Domingo. You must give me location, etc., in order to arrange details of filing, land and mineral right lease, etc. Be careful about the new explosives law, unless you already have a permit.

"Being a woman," reflected Coravel Tio, "she should know that the most important thing in this letter is the very end of it."

He sealed the letter, placed it upon a thick sheaf of bank notes, wrapped the parcel in oiled silk and again in a small waterproof Navaho saddle blanket. This package he gave to the waiting redskin.

"It must go into the hands of that large woman, and no other," he said, gravely. "If you fail, there is trouble for all of us—and perhaps for the gods of the San Marcos also!"

At these last words a flash of keen surprise sprang athwart the Indian's face; then he took the package and turned to the doorway without response. Coravel Tio looked after him, and smiled gently.

CHAPTER IV

MRS. CRUMP HEADS SOUTHWEST

THERE WAS in Domingo a man named Baca. Domingo is a tiny village of adobes nestling along the curve of Santa Fé creek under the gray sharpness of Bajada hill; there is also an Indian pueblo of the same name.

In every ancient native settlement there is at least one man named Baca, which signifies "cow" and may be spelled, in the old fashion, either Baca or Vaca. If these folk came all of one stock, they have increased and multiplied exceedingly.

Under the big cottonwood tree that grew in front of the Baca home sat smoking Joe Gilbert and his partner Lewis. Up to them, and halting abruptly before the house, crept a dust-white flivver in which sat two people: one a woman, great of girth and frame, the other a man, gaunt and haggard, whose black eyes blazed like twin stars of desolation.

The woman alighted and faced the two smokers. They rose and doffed their hats.

"Gents, know where I can find Alf Lewis and Joe Gilbert?" she inquired, bluntly.

"That's us, ma'am."

"Thought so. My name's Mehitabel Crump, with Mrs. for a handle. I'm goin' to open up an ore outcrop. This here is Thady Shea, my partner. Want work, or not?"

"I've heard of you, ma'am," said Gilbert.

"So've I!" exclaimed Lewis. "You bet we want work! Only, ma'am, we'd ought to tell ye square that they's apt to be warrants out for us."

"Warrants never made me lose sleep," said Mrs. Crump, eying them with a nod of satisfaction. "Howsomever, I'll return the favour by saying that if ye take up with me it ain't goin' to be no pleasure trip, gents. 'Cause why, I've got something good, something that'll bring Mackintavers on the trail soon's he smells it—him or his friends. I don't aim to be bluffed out, I don't aim to be bought out, and I don't aim to be lawed out; I got something big, and I aim to hang on to it spite of hell and high water until I sell out big. Them's my openers."

"They're plenty, ma'am," said Gilbert. "We sure would admire to work for you!"

A brief discussion followed as to wages. Thaddeus Roscius Shea sat jack-knifed in the car's front seat, saying not a word. His face was sun-blistered and graven with gnawing desire, his black eyes were feverish, he looked anything but a mining man. Yet the two miners, who must have felt more than a slight curiosity touching him, evinced none. At length Mrs. Crump turned to the car.

"Well, pile in here! Make room in the back, but handle them boxes gentle. Three or four holds blasting powder and dynamite. I had quite a stock left over, and brung it along."

"Do we travel far?" asked Lewis, nervously.

"You bet we do! But don't worry none. I ain't much farther from them boxes than you boys are, and I'm pickin' the soft spots in the road. Besides, I've driv' several hundred mile a'ready with this here outfit, and she ain't gone up on me yet. Barring bad luck, we'd ought to get where we're goin' by the night of day after to-morrow."

"I've heard tell that you had cold iron for nerves," commented Gilbert. "But you ain't backing me down, none whatever, ma'am!"

He sprang in, began to shift the load, and Lewis promptly joined him. Mrs. Crump turned and strode away through the dust. Thady Shea watched her out of sight, then twisted about, and for the first time broke the silence that had enveloped him.

"Gentlemen! May I inquire whether either of you delvers in the deeps of earth are possessed of spirits?"

At the sonorously booming voice Gilbert's jaw dropped in amazement.

"Good gosh! Is that Scripture talk? What d'ye mean—spirits?"

Shea made an impatient gesture. "The fiery fluids that do mingle soul with vaster inspiration! I pray you, give me to drink as you do value drink!"

"Oh, he means a drink!" ejaculated Lewis, staring. "We ain't got a drop, Shea."

The lanky figure jack-knifed together again in disconsolate despair. The two men in the rear of the car glanced at each other. Gilbert tapped his head; Lewis grimaced.

Meantime, Mrs. Crump had passed along the winding row of adobes and finally turned into a corral of high boards. There, concealed from exterior view, she found an automobile at rest; she went on to the adjoining rear door of the adobe house. The door was opened to her by Coravel Tio, who greeted her with a quick smile and a bow.

"My land, it's hot!" said Mrs. Crump. "Howdy!"

"This place is hot indeed," responded the merchant. "Let us take the front room and we may talk in private. I have the papers all made out."

They understood each other very well, these two. Presently, however, Coravel Tio discovered that a third interest in Number Sixteen was to be assigned to Thaddeus Shea, in whose name, also, the entire mining property was to stand. He leaned back and surveyed Mrs. Crump with interest.

"I do not know this man Shea, señora. Why do you make him wealthy?"

There was no hint of offence in his tone. He spoke as one having the right to ask, and Mrs. Crump promptly acquiesced.

"He's an old stage actor, Coravel. I picks him up on the road and takes him along. I'm breakin' him of drink, and I got a hunch that he's goin' to turn out a real man. As for makin' him wealthy, none of us ain't going to thrive on Number Sixteen for quite a spell yet! I'm gambling that Thady Shea will earn all he gets. He's absolutely honest, and good-hearted. He won't know the mine's in his name, and won't care; bein' that way, it'll throw Mackintavers off the track. Besides, I feel downright sorry for Thady; he's had a heap o' misery in his life, looks to me."

The other smiled gently and waved his hand.

"Señora, you are the one woman whose great heart has no equal! It is in my mind that this man will be the cause of misfortune; but what matter? If not from one cause, then from another. Misfortunes are sent by the gods to make us great!

"I shall attend to everything in his name; a good idea, since he will be unknown to Mackintavers or Dorales. You will uncover the vein, and send me more samples immediately. These other two men must become small shareholders, so that adjacent claims and mining rights may be secured for the company. Once we are secure, we may talk of eastern capital."

"Once we're secure," said Mrs. Crump grimly, "look out for Mackintavers, then and before; likewise, after!"

"Exactly." Coravel Tio bowed and finished his writing.

A little later Mrs. Crump shook hands with him and departed. Coravel Tio watched her off, and heard the roar of her car's engine. The roar became a thrum that lessened and died into the distance like a droning fly. Only then, it seemed, a sudden thought shook the man.

"*Dios*—I forgot!" he ejaculated. "I forgot to ask her about the permit for the explosives! Well, I warned her in the note. What matter? These incidents of destiny are intended to work out their own effects, and good somehow comes from everything. I am a philosopher!"

Blissfully unconscious whether philosophy might be of aid in running a flivver, Mrs. Crump headed southward over the river road to Albuquerque.

A rough road is that, and well travelled. Mrs. Crump was in some haste to get over this section unobserved, and it was entirely evident that her haste was greater than her caution regarding the jiggling boxes in the rear of the car.

More than once the two men in the tonneau stared quickly at each other's white faces; more than once the boxes and bundles crashed and banged fearsomely, in view of their partial contents; but Mrs. Crump only threw in more gas and plunged ahead. As for Thaddeus Roscius Shea, he stared out upon the passing scenery with glazed and lack-lustre eyes, and held his peace.

When at last they arrived in the outskirts of Albuquerque, Mrs. Crump paused at a wayside station to fill up with oil and gasoline, also to refill several emptied water bags which formed part of the equipment.

"We ain't goin' into town," she vouchsafed, curtly, to her charges. "And when we gets reaching out over the mesa, you two boys act tender with them boxes! They's two-three places we got to ford cattle runs, and we got to do it sudden to keep out of the quicksands. But don't worry no more, there ain't no special danger."

The advice was entirely superfluous. Gilbert and Lewis could by no means have worried more. They had reached the limit.

Barely skimming the outlying streets of Albuquerque, Mrs. Crump avoided the better-known highway beside the railroad and took the shorter but deserted road that leads south over the mesa to Becker. Most of this was covered before darkness descended upon them.

Then a brief and barren camp was made; it was also a fireless camp, and the "grub" was cold. Stiff and weary though the three passengers were, it was clearly impossible that they should prove less tough than a mere woman. So, when after an hour's halt Mrs. Crump grimly cranked up, they piled into the car without protest.

On they went through the darkness. It was well after midnight when the iron nature of Mehitabel Crump acknowledged signs of approaching dissolution in the hand that rocked the steering wheel. Admitting her weakness with a sigh, she turned out of the interminable road and halted. Blanket rolls were unlashed, and sleep descended swiftly upon three members of that quartet.

It must be told that this camp was a milepost in the life of Thaddeus Roscius Shea. He could not sleep. A hundred yards away from the camp he strode up and down under the cold stars, his gaunt body shivering with the chill of the night, his haggard features contorted with the desperate anguish of shattered nerves. All the old impertinences of his soul were risen strong within him; he wanted to run away and end this intolerable situation. He wanted to run away, here and now!

Yet, when at length he clumsily wrapped himself in his blanket and fell asleep, tears beaded his hollow cheeks and reflected the pale starlight above; and like the stars, those tears were cleansing, and serenely sad. The first tears he had shed in years—the tears of a man, wrung from deep within him; tears of brief conquest over himself. He would stick!

Sunrise found the dust-white flivver once more far afield.

The remaining details of that odyssey have no place here. The dust-white flivver came safely to its destination, and work duly began upon Number Sixteen. Days of hard, back-breaking labour ensued—days in which living quarters had to be erected before the claim could be touched. In those days Thaddeus Roscius Shea became, for good and all, Thady Shea.

Number Sixteen lay among the most desolate of desolate hills, just over the ridge of a long hogback. In the cañon below there was a trickle of water from the mountains; beside this *rito* were erected two rough shacks, and here the dust-white flivver rested peacefully. To the north towered the higher forested ranges whence came the cañon—the continental divide, rugged crests leaping at the sky. Below, a few miles distant, stretched the bad lands and the lava beds; a scoriated, blasphemous strip such as is often found in the southwest. Behind this lay scattered ranches and the road into Zacaton City.

Up on that hogback, leaning upon his pick, stood Thady Shea. Gone was the threadbare black raiment, gone and replaced by overalls, high boots, flannel shirt. Shea was less conscious of his changed exterior than were those about him. Lewis and Gilbert, preparing a blasting charge a hundred feet distant, glanced at the great, gaunt figure.

"Bloomed out most amazing, ain't he?" said Lewis. "No tinhorn, neither. Dead game."

Gilbert, cutting the fuse with deft fingers, wagged his head. "Sure looks that-a-way, partner. Reckon Mis' Crump knew her business, after all, when she tied up with him. Gosh! Ain't she one a-gile critter, though?"

Shea stood rocklike, watching the blast. Even in this short space of time the swing of axe and pick had hardened him amazingly; his towering figure seemed to move with a more lissome flow of muscles; for the first time in his life, most wonderful of all, his deeply lined features had become centred about one fixed and determined purpose—to keep himself clean of liquor. He had conquered, and with the victory had come a new serenity.

The muffled report of the blast echoed dully. From nowhere appeared Mrs. Crump, hastily coming to the scene. Shea dropped his pick and joined the others. Mrs. Crump, examining the results of the blast, flung out an exultant cry.

"Got it!"

"Ain't much of a vein," observed Gilbert, skeptically. "Veins, rather—looks like a lot of 'em, and they go deep. This here limestone runs clear to Chiny, I reckon."

Mrs. Crump chuckled in a satisfied manner.

"These here veins don't never come big, Gilbert. Who'd think this here greenish-white stuff was better'n a gold seam? But she is. Well, never mind any more work a while, boys. I got a letter already writ, and when I fill in the size o' these here openings, she's ready to mail—and she's got to be sent sudden. These samples likewise.

"Let's see; I ain't goin' to town myself. Mackintavers' men are sure to be watchin' everywhere, and this here location has got to be kept secret if possible. I s'pose the devils will get it from the land office, though. Joe, can you and Al show up in Zacaton City without occasioning no rumpus?"

Gilbert shook his head doubtfully.

"I reckon not, ma'am. We're pretty well known there, and we ain't right sure how things is fixed for us. Still, it won't bother us none; if you say so, we'll go—"

"Nope; can't take no chances with the letter and samples, boys. It's up to Thady. He's learned how to run the car, anyhow. Thady, you got to send them samples and a letter. No one's goin' to suspect you of bein' partners with me, and be sure to send the samples in your own name, savvy?

"They's enough gas to take you into Zacaton, and ye can bring a fresh supply when ye come back. Then we need more flour an' grub, for which same I got a list made out already. A new axe helve, too. Don't forget that there axe helve, whatever ye do! It ain't on the list—I guess ye can remember it all right. Sure, now! Don't come without it. How soon can ye get going?"

"Now," said Shea, a slight smile curving his wide lips.

CHAPTER V

THE AMBITION OF MACKINTAVERS

I T I S an established but peculiar trait of human nature, by which most of us desire to be that which we are not, or to do that for which we have no talent. I, who write, may aspire to be a great engineer; you, who read, may aspire to the study of the stars. We reach out toward that which we may never grasp.

Sandy Mackintavers was a wealthy and a powerful man; his hands were gripped hard in both the politics and the mining properties of the state. Self-made and self-educated, he had accomplished a good job of it. He had, of necessity, seen a good deal of those men who were ever radiating out from Santa Fé; those men who, on behalf of many universities and great museums, were ever delving amid the thousands of pre-historic ruins which lay in and between the valleys of the Pecos and the Rio Grande.

Slowly, Sandy had discovered that these men were digging in the earth for science, and that science and the world of letters honoured them. He had learned something of their "patter" and of the things they were seeking; he had studied their work and methods and ideals, and he had found within himself the makings of a scientist. In short, he had formed the stupendous ambition of becoming, at one fell stroke, a renowned ethnologist!

Do not smile. In the course of thirty years a man can pick up a great many divers things, and it was the way of Mackintavers to pick up everything in sight. Sandy knew a great deal more than he appeared to know. He had mining properties all over, and he was a silent partner in a chain of Mormon trading stores that ran north from the Mexican border through three states. His sources of information were varied.

Being unmarried and loving his ease when he was in the city, Mackintavers maintained a suite at the Aztec House. He had entertained many men in that place, some to their eternal sorrow. Never had he entertained a more distinguished visitor, however, than the Smithsonian professor with whom he was speaking on this Sunday morning—a scientist known around the world, and a man of supreme authority in ethnologic circles.

"Now, professor," said Mackintavers, bluntly, "I ain't a college-educated man, but I've knocked around this country for thirty year, and I know a few things. When I die, I aim to be remembered as something more than a mining man, see?"

The other, in puzzled suspense, nodded tacit understanding.

"Now," pursued Sandy, chewing hard on a cigar, "if I had something to give the Smithsonian or some other museum, something that would be a tenstrike for science, something that

'ud make every scientific shark in the country water at the eyes
for envy, what 'ud the Smithsonian do for *me?*"

The professor cleared his throat and registered hesitation.

"I—ah—I do not exactly apprehend your meaning, Mr.
Mackintavers. You do not speak in a financial sense, I presume?"

"Of course not. I tell you, I want to be known as a scientist!
Man, I've got the biggest thing up my sleeve that you ever
struck! Can your museum, or any other, make me famous as a
scientist? That is, if I turn over a regular tenstrike?"

"Ah—that is exceedingly difficult to answer. A scientific
reputation, Mr. Mackintavers, is founded upon solid bases, upon
research or discoveries. If your—ah—contribution were a thing
of such merit as you say, it would undoubtedly be published far
and wide. Your name, naturally, would be attached to it, according as your work justified."

"In other words," amended Sandy, "if I turn over a complete
job, I'd get full credit and publicity?"

"Yes."

"That's what I want. I'm interested in this ethnology stuff,
and I can do you sharks a whopping good turn. I want to get
the credit, that's all. Folks call me a hard-fisted old mining crab,
and I want to show 'em that I'm something more."

"A highly laudable ambition, sir. You understand, however,
that what to a lay mind might appear to be a most interesting
ethnological fact, to a scientist might prove well known or
insufficiently supported—"

Mackintavers waved his square hand.

"This thing is all assayed and fire tested, professor, and I'm
no fool. May I give you an outline of it?"

"If you care to, by all means do so!"

"You know where the San Marcos pueblo is—away down
south of Bonanza?" Mackintavers struck into his subject without
further parley. "It was abandoned about 1680 because of attacks
from the Comanches, who destroyed several pueblos down in
that country. There's a tradition that the Injuns migrated west

of the Rio Grande and settled the Cochiti and Domingo pueblos. Has that tradition ever been proved up?"

The professor evinced an awakening interest.

"No, sir. We know that the survivors of the Pecos pueblo went to Jimez, but the older migrations are hidden in the mists of time, unfortunately. Where the present Pueblos came from we do not know. The migrations—"

"They won't be hid very long," said Mackintavers, complacently. "Aiblins, now, we'll clear 'em up a bit, eh?"

The only Scottish evidences which remained from Sandy's youth were an uncanny acquisitiveness and a habit of interjecting the word "aiblins" into the conversation at random. When Sandy used that word, it betrayed mental effort.

"Some time ago," he resumed, "a man found seven stone idols in a bit of the adobe ruins at San Marcos. They had been walled up and buried alive, ye might say. The heavy rains last year, which took out some pieces of the adobe walls, washed 'em out. I've got 'em now, down to my ranch near Magdalena."

At this announcement the professor displayed mild disappointment. He had been more than interested in Sandy's preamble, but this supposed climax caused him to shake his gray head regretfully.

"My dear sir, these idols are of course very rare things, but not exceptionally so. I fail to see how they would give any proof of migration—"

"Hold on; I ain't done yet! A drunken Injun from Cochiti seen those idols and spilled a good deal of information, calling them by name and so on. That is not evidence which would stand on a scientific basis, I reckon. But if a Cochiti man could be made to talk, and if he was to recognize those idols first crack as his ancestral gods—"

"And not be drunk at the time," interjected the other, smiling.

"Sure. If he was to name 'em like old friends, and they corresponded with the same idols from Cochiti which are in various museums—then wouldn't all this go to show mighty plain that the migration theory was true?"

Mackintavers leaned back, breathless and triumphant. The scientist nodded quickly.

"Sir, this is an unusual and surprising proposal, but I cannot deny your premises. I do believe that such evidence would go a long way, could it be secured. That, of course, is the doubtful point, for these red men can very seldom be made to talk. However, you have an astounding perception of ethnologic values in merely conceiving the scheme!"

"Taken by and large, that's nothing but human nature. Well?"

"If this proof could really be adduced, it would be epochal! The possibilities, sir, would be tremendous in their application!"

"It ain't proved up yet," returned Sandy, drily, "but it will be. It may take a bit of time gettin' things in shape—a week or so, maybe. Ye know, professor, these Injuns are touchy about questions o' deity, and they have to be handled wi' gloves. But I'll do it! A bag of silver dollars will loom mighty big to them. If ye care to be on hand when the time comes, I'd be glad to have ye as a guest at my ranch—"

In many ways the professor had an extended knowledge of New Mexico. It is quite possible that he knew all about the playful habits of Sandy Mackintavers in regard to testimony along mining and mineral lines. So, while he did not restrain his enthusiasm over the ambition of his host, he made it plain that he certainly did wish to be on hand when the testimony in this case was obtained.

Mackintavers agreed readily, for in this instance he was more or less resolved to play fair; and the interview ended.

Scarcely had the scientist departed, than the door opened to admit an individual of striking appearance. This gentleman was the satellite, the adherent, and field marshal, the *âme damnée*, of Mackintavers.

Mormon progenitors had given him a stocky, massive front and splendid build, a steely eye and projecting lower jaw. A

touch of Mexican blood had given him coarse black hair, a swart
complexion, and sinister mental attributes. He had much the
appearance of a west-coast Irishman, with his black hair and
gray eyes, but there the resemblance ended. Such was Abel
Dorales, a man of reputation and education.

"Well?" greeted Mackintavers, abruptly. "What's up now?"

"Trouble," was the response. "Rodrigo Cota wants to see you.
Also, I got a telegram from Ben Aimes, at Zacaton City, but
haven't decoded it yet. I think it's about the Crump woman."

"Then hurry it along," snapped Mackintavers. "Send Cota in
here pronto."

A moment later entered the room a nervous native, the same
legislator who had briefly interviewed Coravel Tio regarding
the moving of the capital. Mr. Cota stood mopping his brow
and glancing around.

"Well, Cota?" exploded Sandy, transfixing him with frowning gaze. "What's the matter now? Need more money to swing
it?"

"Señor," blurted the legislator in desperation, "it cannot be
swung!"

"Oh! And why not, Mr. Cota?"

"I do not know. Three weeks ago we had a clear majority. The
measure was to be presented to-morrow—but our men have
gone to pieces!"

"Do they want more money?" snapped Sandy, savagely.

The native shrugged. "I have done my best! It is a question
of the people. In some way, I know not how, word has been
spread abroad that the capital is to be changed. Our people are
furious. Our natives, sir, have sentiment about this—"

"Sentiment, hell!" snarled Mackintavers, as his fist crashed
down. "I tell ye, it's goin' to be done! Ain't there plenty in it for
all, ye fool? Ain't new state buildings got to be built at Albuquerque? Ain't—"

"Señor, it is no question of money; it cannot be done! I myself dare not propose this bill without voting for it; and I cannot vote for it."

"Why not?" The face of Mackintavers was purpled, seething with furious passions. Livid, the native glared back at him.

"Because I am afraid for my life."

Mackintavers leaped to his feet in a whirlwind of rage at what he considered a palpable lie. The native shrank back, but doggedly, as though a greater fear were beside him than any fear of this political master of his.

At this instant the door opened and Abel Dorales appeared. He made a slight gesture, a gesture of command, of authority. The empurpled countenance of Mackintavers composed itself by a mighty effort.

"Very well, Mr. Cota," he said, thickly. "Let the bill pass over for this time, since I got more important business on hand than chasing down you native senators. But let me tell you this: When it comes up again, there'll be no more talk like you've just handed out—or I'll know the reason why. Get out!"

Cota took his hat and left, thankfully. Dorales closed the door, while a flood of oaths burst from the lips of Mackintavers. With extended hand, Dorales checked the flood.

"Never mind that, Sandy," he said, calmly. "We'll probably find later that the railroad is double-crossing us. There's no rush—we can get to the bottom of it in time. The more important affair is this of the Crump woman, so far as money goes. There's a bigger fortune in this mine than in any political game!"

Uncouth bear that he was, Mackintavers could be swayed by this more polished tongue; he knew this tongue was devoted absolutely to his own interests, and he forced himself to accept the dictum of Dorales at the moment.

"Well?" he growled. "Ye don't mean to say she's down at Zacaton?"

"The wire was from your store manager there, Aimes. He said merely that he had smashed the Crump outfit flat, and that I had better get there in a hurry to take charge of things."

"Aiblins, yes!" The thin lips of Sandy curled back. "We hadn't looked for such quick action, Abel. That Aimes is a good man! I s'pose this news don't grieve ye none, after what the lady done to you. How's your head?"

A fleeting contraction passed across the face of Dorales. His eyes narrowed to thin slits. His nose quivered like the nose of a dog sniffing game.

"Thank you, it's quite well," his voice was low and cruel. "If you think best, I shall go down there immediately."

Mackintavers crammed a cigar between his teeth and chewed at it for a moment.

"Aiblins, yes," he mused aloud. "Somebody has blocked us on this moving-the-capital bill. I won't get hold of the skunk right away, neither; we might's well call it off until the next session.

"Tell ye what, Abel! I'm fixing to spend a while at my ranch, so I'll go south with ye. I'll need ye mighty bad to get that business of the Injun gods moving along, because I got my heart set on doin' that up brown. But as ye say, this mine means millions—the biggest strike in the state in a long time. The assayer was positive it was strontianite and not merely barytes?"

"Dead certain," assented Dorales.

"Well, it won't be such a long job; I'll be at the ranch where ye can reach me quick. We'll have to find out what Aimes has done, then make plans and go ahead. If there's one thing that the Lord gave me ability to do, it was to handle mining deals!"

"With a cold deck," added Dorales. "Very well. If we go by auto, we can save a good deal of time."

Mackintavers grimaced. "I ain't built for long trips, but go ahead. Get the big car, Abel. Want to run her yourself? All right. Land me at the ranch, then go on to Zacaton City with the ranch flivver, unless ye want the big car."

"The flivver is the thing down there."

"Aiblins, yes. And mind! What we got to do is to get that Crump female clear off'n her location; that's all. Aimes has evidently found some means of gettin' her arrested. We can take that for granted. By the time you get there, she'll be in the calaboose.

"You telephone me at the ranch with a full account of what's happened, and I'll have a scheme ready for ye. The main thing is to get possession of the property; maybe we can frame a deal on this fellow Shea—it's all held in his name, ain't it? That was a foxy move, but not foxy enough to fool us long! Get possession, Abel, and the law will do the rest for us."

"It ought to!" Dorales showed white and even teeth as he smiled.

Mackintavers met those steely eyes beneath their strangely black brows, and his square mouth unfolded in a grin.

"Get possession, that's all!" he uttered.

"Consider it done, Sandy. If you'll be ready in an hour, I'll be around with the car."

CHAPTER VI

THADY SHEA SMELLS WHISKEY

THE LITTLE town of Zacaton City, within easy trucking distance of the railroad, formed the nucleus of a goodly mining centre. Its residential section was extensive, and consisted of adobes occupied by "native" miners or workmen. Its business section was made up chiefly of a bank, the Central Mercantile Store, hardware, drug, and harness shops, and a soda-water parlour that adjoined the Central Mercantile. This last was a blind pig, maintained with circumspection and profit by Ben Aimes, manager of the store. Aimes also ran the combination hotel-garage across the street.

Thady Shea came into town about sunset. He had broken bread on the way, and disdained to seek further dinner. Having been much cautioned, he was wary of danger. Leaving the dust-white flivver at the garage, he went to the express office and sent off his ore samples and letter, then he sought the emporium of Ben Aimes.

The two native clerks being busy, Aimes, a brisk fellow of thirty, espied the tall figure of Shea, and in person took charge of the customer.

"Well, partner, what can I do for you?" he inquired, cheerfully. "Can't say as I've seen you before. Stranger in town?"

Shea fumbled in his pocket for the list of supplies, and transfixed the merchant with his cavernous black eyes. He had been particularly warned against Aimes.

"Friend," he trumpeted, "you say sooth. Truth sits upon thy lips, marry it does!"

Aimes blinked rapidly. "Stranger, I don't get you! You're a prospector?"

"That, sir, is somewhat of my present business," boomed Shea. "Yet have I seen the day when every room hath blazed with lights and brayed with minstrelsy, when thick-eyed musing and cursed melancholy fled from before me like twin evil spirits! Make ready, friend, thy pencil for its task."

Those sonorous tones drew grinning attention from others. Aimes, quite overcome by the rounded periods and the imposing gestures, asked no more questions, but devoted himself to making ready packages as Shea read off from his list the supplies required.

Two or three loafers sauntered along and listened to Shea's enunciation with awed delight. When the end of the list was reached, the amounts totalled, and the money handed over, Thady Shea carelessly crumpled up the list and tossed it behind the counter.

His arms filled with the bundles, he left the store and crossed the street to his car. He had laid up the flivver for the night, and now attended to having it filled with gas and oil. He stated to the mechanic that he might be here for several days; at this juncture, it occurred to him that he had forgotten that axe helve which Mrs. Crump had demanded especially.

Meantime, Ben Aimes had retrieved the list of supplies, and had stared at the uncrumpled paper with amazed recognition. He swiftly summoned one of the idling loafers.

"If this ain't the writing of Mrs. Crump, I'm a liar! You chase over to the garage and get the number o' that feller's car—hump, now!"

Thady Shea reëntered the store, in blissful ignorance that he was done for, and demanded his axe helve. Ben Aimes, in blissful ignorance of what that axe helve was destined to mean to him and to others, filled the order. Then, handling Shea his change, Aimes gave him a meaning wink.

"Step into the sody parlour a minute, stranger! Have a cigar on the store."

The offer was entirely innocuous. Shea greatly desired to avoid any argument or trouble, so he followed Aimes into the adjoining room, which at this hour was deserted. Aimes procured cigars, then went to the soda fountain.

"Want you to try somethin' new we got here," he said, and paused. "What did you say your name was?"

"My cognomen, sir, is Shea. Thaddeus Shea."

"Well, Shea, just hold this under your nose and see if it smells like sody."

Unsuspicious as any innocent, Shea took the proffered glass and held it to his nose. A tremor ran through him—an uncontrollable shiver that sent fever into his eyes. He lowered the glass slightly and forced a ghastly smile. Already defeat had engulfed him.

"Friend, I am sorry thus to disappoint you, but I have sworn that never—"

"Shucks!" Aimes grinned and held up his own glass. To meet it, that of Shea again came within sniffing distance. "Just one between business acquaintances, Mr. Shea. It's the finest licker ever got to this city! Absolutely twenty year old, partner. One little snifter now—don't it smell good? The real thing, the real thing!"

Thady Shea's entire system was impregnated by that whiff. His big fingers closed upon the little glass with a convulsive contraction.

"One, sir, and one only!" he declaimed. "To the dead god Bacchus, all hail!"

He tossed down the drink and smacked his lips.

It was upon a Saturday evening that these things happened. That smell had done the business for Thady Shea; that raw odour of whiskey, which in a flash had permeated to the very deeps of his being with its awful lure. No guile, no argument could have forced him to drink, but that sniff had ruined him utterly.

Twenty minutes later, in maudlin confidence, he was relating to Ben Aimes how two miners of his acquaintance had driven several hundred miles in deadly fear of being hoisted by dynamite at every jolt.

Shea mentioned no names. Drunk or not, he knew subconsciously that he must mention no names. Also subconsciously, he knew that he must hang on to his axe helve or Mrs. Crump would be much disappointed in him. So he was still hanging on to it when, after a parting drink, he was thrust forth into the cold night air. That parting drink had been soggy with opiates.

Ben Aimes went to the telephone and called up the sheriff at Silver City.

"This is Aimes at Zacaton, Bill," he said. "A queer guy just blew in here to-night with a grand souse and is sleeping it off now. You know old lady Crump, don't you? Heard of her at any rate. Well, he says that she's out in the hills a piece with two other fellers. These two were run out o' Magdalena last month for talking agin' the gov'ment and they're said to be dangerous characters. The place is north o' the bad lands, over in Socorro County.

"The p'int is, Bill, this here guy says they've got heap o' dynamite and such stuff out there. Them two anarchists ought to be prevented usin' it; according to this guy, they got no licenses and never heard o' the new license law. This here is plumb illegal and you'd ought to stop it. Both these fellers are I. W. W. organizers, he says, and prob'ly are German spies; this guy talked with a queer kind of accent.

"No, I wouldn't think it o' Mrs. Crump, neither, but you never can tell these days. What's that? Well, I got the location pretty straight from this guy. Yep, a car can make it; he come into town that way. Get up on the night train and you can take my car out there. Sure, I'll meet the train. You're welcome."

This pleasant duty finished, Aimes dispatched a lengthy telegram to Abel Dorales at Santa Fé. He then summoned the constable in search of Thady Shea. But Shea had vanished from human ken, although the dust-white flivver remained in the garage.

Bright and early next morning Aimes departed in his automobile, went to the railroad and met the sheriff, and brought that official back to town. The hardware merchant was pressed into service as a deputy, and the sheriff took over Aimes' car.

"I'd like to go along myself," said Aimes, regretfully, "but I got to 'tend the garridge myself to-day account of my mechanic hurting himself last night and being laid up. Tell ye what, Bill! Why not take the whole crowd right down to Silver City? It'll save ye comin' back here, and your new deppity yonder can fetch the car back here. Sure, you're dead welcome! I ain't got no use for the car anyhow."

To this arrangement the sheriff consented gladly, and Aimes watched them depart with a twinkle in his eye. Before Mrs. Crump could possibly return from Silver City, to say nothing of her two men, Abel Dorales would be on the spot to take charge of things. Aimes considered that he had managed things very neatly indeed, and he mentally patted himself on the back that morning.

Ben Aimes, however, did not take local politics into account. It is such little unconsidered trifles which very often go to make up the warp of affairs of larger moment.

Only a few months previously an ancient and honourable gentleman by the name of Ferris had been ousted from the job of justice of the peace, mainly on account of certain hostility to Ben Aimes and the Mackintavers forces. It is quite possible that old man Ferris was no good as a justice, yet he had an inconspicuous but important part to play in the tangled affairs of Thady Shea and Sandy Mackintavers, to say nothing of the seven stone gods.

In broad daylight, therefore, Thady Shea came to his senses. While slow remembrance dawned upon him, he found himself reposing in the back yard of an adobe house; how he got there was never explained. A furred tongue and an aching head gradually brought home some errant sense of shame. This feeling was intensified by a goat-like visage above him.

"Well, pilgrim!" sounded a raucous voice. "Slep' it off, have ye?"

Shea groaned and sat up. "Where—where am I?"

"Town of Zacaton City, county o' Grant, State o' New Mexico." The other chuckled. He was a disreputable old fellow, distinguished by shiftless garb and dirty gray hair. "I reckon Ben Aimes must have give ye quite a jag, eh? If I was you, I'd spill out o' town right smart. He's got the constable lookin' for ye."

Shea clasped his head and groaned again, not understanding the words clearly.

"I've fallen!" he moaned.

"With a thud," agreed the other. "But worse'n that, pilgrim. Ye've gone and got ol' Mis' Crump in real bad. If ye wasn't so mis'able I'd boot ye out o' here for it."

Thady Shea stared up dully. "What—what's that you say?"

Old man Ferris surveyed him in pitying contempt, and carefully sank his remaining fangs into a plug of tobacco.

"D'ye mean as ye don't know what ye been an' done? Well, I can't say as I can see why Mis' Crump ever's taken up with the likes of you, but it's plumb certain that ye've gone an' done for her this trip, ye no-account swine!"

Shea's brow broke into cold perspiration. His quickening faculties began to grasp the sense of these words.

"Expound!" he said. "What have I done?"

"A plenty. The sheriff come over this mornin'. Him and a deppity has gone to arrest Mis' Crump—and all along o' you, ye mis'able coyote!"

"Arrest her? Why?" Shea stared, his heart sinking. So piteous was his gaze that old man Ferris turned aside, spat, and resumed his discourse in kindlier tones.

"Don't ye know that they's a new law about explosives? Well, they is. Everybody what handles powder or dynamite has got to have a license. From what I gather, Mis' Crump ain't wise to it and ain't got none.

"Last night you done blabbed out your soul to Aimes. Danged fool! Why did Aimes git the sheriff after Mis' Crump? Ain't but one answer to that—so's that devil Mackintavers could profit! And sheriff's goin' to take 'em to Silver City, too. If Mis' Crump has located an ore prop'ty, as looks likely, Mackintavers is after it.

"Once she gits out'n the way and they ain't nobody to hold down the location, some o' Mackintavers' crowd is going to jump it sure's shooting! Huh! Git out'n my back yard 'fore I come back, ye swine!"

Snorting angrily, old man Ferris turned and stamped away, and so out of the story. He had fulfilled his share in destiny, with greater measure than he knew.

Thady Shea sat staring, his eyes terrible with comprehension. With every moment that final exposition sank more deeply into his brain. The ghastly consequences of his own weakness left him stunned and paralyzed.

He could dimly remember what had happened, up to that final drink. He was certain that he had not mentioned the name of Mehitabel Crump. Yet he could remember telling about those explosives; as he connected things, he groaned again. Aimes had been pumping him, of course; had somehow suspected something.

The pitiless deduction of old man Ferris struck upon Shea's brain like a trip-hammer. The mine was left unprotected, or soon would be, and Mackintavers' men would grab it. Of course!

Frightful remorse crumpled Thady Shea, mentally and bodily. He owed all that he was, all that he might be, to Mrs. Crump; yet his action had literally ruined her. That cursed sniff of whiskey had done it! Shea wasted no recrimination upon himself for his lapse from rectitude. He had gone through all that before. It was the consequence of this lapse that horrified him, that lashed down upon his soul.

"What have I done!" he mumbled, groping for coherency. "What have I done!"

All the old memories of Mrs. Crump flooded into his mind. He recalled all her actions and words, he pictured mentally all the deep waters of human kindness that lay hidden below her mask of harshness, he visioned anew how she had picked him out of the very gutter and had set him upon his feet, a man. How had he repaid her?

In this hour Thady Shea was cast absolutely upon himself. There was none to whom he might go for advice or aid. He was alone with his consciousness of guilt, alone with the remorse that ate into his heart like acid. A month previously he would have mouthed a curse at the world and have gone shambling away in search of the nearest saloon, where he would have recited "The Face on the Barroom Floor" as the sure and certain price of liquor.

This thought recurred to him. He pictured himself as he was a month ago. From his lips was wrenched an inarticulate cry, the voice of a soul in anguish. Heedless of the burning ache in his head, he brought his long body erect and looked up at the sky.

"Oh, God!" he said, a dry sob in his throat. "Oh, God! I have scoffed and blasphemed because You let me stumble down into hell. It was my own fault, God. Now, for the sake of that woman who helped me to find myself, it's up to You to give me a hand! I don't know what to do. But I've got to make up for this thing that I've done, and there is no one to help me except You—and it's for her sake—"

The words failed, for as he spoke out his heart the deepness of feeling that had laid hold upon him ebbed; just as the bitterness of grief ebbs with tears. A tremor shook him, and for a moment he stood motionless.

Close at hand was an *acequia,* an open ditch with running water. He went to it, kneeled, and plunged his head into the water; it cooled his brain and steadied him. He rose and saw his axe helve lying where he had lain that night. He picked it up and stood there, indecision eating into him.

What was to be done? He must do something. The constable was seeking him—why? No matter. The name of Ben Aimes explained everything. The morning was wearing along, and by this time all hope of warning Mrs. Crump was gone. Of course, there was the dust-white flivver. He could take that and sneak back to the mine. It would be deserted.

Deserted? But that was what Mackintavers wanted, according to this disreputable ancient! That was why Mrs. Crump was under arrest! That was the aim and purpose of the whole affair—to have the mine left deserted, so that the man Dorales could step in and seize upon it.

The gaunt, grim face of Shea tightened and hardened. "One thing I can do—go there," he reflected. "What the hell have I to worry about—can they do any worse to me than I have done to myself? No. They'll try to arrest me, they'll try to keep me here. They can't do it! I'm going."

As he left the place and sought the road, there was a sublime unconsciousness of self in him. He was in no condition of mind to do the usual, the conventional thing, the thing that any sane man would have done, the thing that any one would be expected to do.

No! From that hour, Shea was a different man. He had entered upon this new and primitive existence, and now it took hold upon him. His course of life had been abruptly shifted, and he was climbing new paths; as he climbed, the exhilaration of the heights sang in his blood. He had flung away the lessons of his old dreary years. Now his actions were to be the simple, terrible, and impulsive actions of a child who fears no consequences.

Finding that he was only a couple of blocks from the main street of the town, Shea walked toward it, the axe helve still in his hand. He meant to take out his flivver and go.

There was no church in Zacaton City, and it was not yet time for the Mormon chapel to open. The garage doors were wide. In front, standing in the warm sunlight, Ben Aimes was chatting with the constable about the mysterious disappearance of the man Shea. Half-a-dozen idlers were lined up to one side, smoking and discussing the coming and going of the sheriff. Around the corner of the store, across the street, swung the gaunt figure of Shea.

"By gosh!" exclaimed Aimes, staring. He clutched the arm of the constable. "There's the cuss now! Lay him up until Dorales gets here to-morrow, anyhow. Whew! I'm glad he's showed up at last. Must ha' been laying in a ditch."

The loafers galvanized into sudden interest. The constable started across the street and met Shea midway. He held out one hand, with the other showing his badge of office.

"Get out of my way," said Shea, lifelessly, looking through him.

"None o' that, now," snorted the constable. "You come along with me."

With a smack that was heard for half a block, the axe helve swung a vicious half-circle and landed over the officer's ear. The constable threw out his hands and fell on his face, lying motionless. Shea strode forward.

"Lay on to him, boys, he's locoed!" cried Aimes, turning to the men behind. He whirled again to face Shea, and his right hand crept to his hip. "Hello, Shea! lay down that—"

"You gave me a drink last night, didn't you?" said Shea, halting before him.

Aimes laughed, thinking that he perceived what was in the other's mind.

"Oh, want another, do ye?" he returned. "Well, lay down that—"

"You're the man that gave me a drink," said Shea. His deep bass voice boomed upon the morning air like a bell. "If any man dares to give me a drink again, he'll get worse than this."

Aimes suddenly perceived danger, and whipped out his weapon. Swifter than his hand was the axe helve. It struck his wrist and knocked the revolver away. As he staggered to the blow, the axe helve swung again and smote him over the head. Aimes made a queer noise in his throat and limply sank down.

There was something frightful in the deliberate way those two men had been felled. For a moment Shea stood gazing at the loafers, who shrank back before his blazing eyes. Then:

"I'll do worse than this to any man who dares give me a drink again," he said.

Without further heed, he passed into the garage. Up and down the street men were calling, running. The group outside the place looked at each other, their faces blanched.

"My Lord!" gasped someone. "He's done killed 'em both! In after him, boys."

Thady Shea laid down his bludgeon in front of the dust-white flivver, and began to crank. For almost the first time in his life he had struck a man in cold anger; more terrible than this thought, however, was the acid-like bitterness in his soul.

Just as the engine caught and roared, Shea, rising, saw over his shoulder the string of men pouring in upon him. He had no time to get into his car. With a quick motion he caught up the axe helve; swiftly the foremost men flung themselves upon him, and found him facing them.

There in the obscurity of the little garage ensued a scene that is still told of from Silver City to Magdalena. All noise was drowned in the roar of the engine that throbbed behind Shea. Outside, other men paused to ask what was going on, to group about the figures of Aimes and the constable. Inside, Shea fought for more than his life.

There were six men against him; yet, in the felling of those two outside, the battle had been half won, for the cold terror of Shea's blows had made itself felt. The first man at him shrieked out and fell, crawling away with a broken arm. The others came in before Shea could recover from the blow, and fastened upon him like dogs upon a mountain lion.

Silent, deadly, Shea swung up his weapon and waited. He took their blows without return. He braced himself against the throbbing car behind him, and awaited his time. Then he began to strike. There was nothing blind and frantic in his blows; rather there was something fearful and inhuman, for inside him was that which rendered him insensible to the smiting fists, and when he brought down his weapon it was with simple and deadly intent.

Three times he struck, each time lifting on his toes, and twice lifting one man who had fastened about his waist. To his three blows, a man reeled away into the darkness; a second plunged forward beneath an adjacent car; a third ran screaming into the open air, across his face a bloody blotch. A fourth man, unhurt, turned and ran.

Shea looked down, curiously, at the last assailant, who was still gripping him around the waist, trying to bend him backward. Then he deliberately heaved up his axe helve and brought down the rounded oval of the halt against the man's head twice. At the second crunching blow the man's grip relaxed. Shea threw him, staggering and clutching, clear across the garage floor, then turned and leaped into his car.

With a grinding roar and a honk of the horn, the dust-white flivver went out of the wide-open doorway into the street.

Men jumped aside, yelled, pursued. Somebody fired a revolver, and the bullet smashed the windshield in front of Shea's face. Other shots sounded, but flew wild. The car went around the nearest corner on two wheels, and shot away toward the west at thirty miles an hour.

Thady Shea had come and gone.

CHAPTER VII

THADY SHEA HAS A VISITOR

THADY SHEA was on his way to Number Sixteen. The sheriff was on his way to Silver City with Mrs. Crump, Gilbert, and Lewis. In the ordinary course of events, Thady Shea would have encountered them in the cañon north of No Agua. The ordinary course of events did not obtain, however, because of Ben Aimes.

Having sustained nothing worse than a broken wrist and a sore head, Ben Aimes upon being revived at once telephoned the store and post office at No Agua to stop Thady Shea. No Agua was the jumping-off place at the edge of the bad lands, and it was nothing but a long frame building from which radiated all the cañon trails to north and west.

When Shea arrived, he found a reception committee awaiting him in the shape of a dozen men, most of whom were mounted upon horses or mules as if they had convened for a Sunday holiday. Shea needed no information upon the subject of his reception. He had previously observed the telephone wires and had drawn his own conclusions. As he drew near to No Agua he was the recipient of a bullet that finished off the windshield and sent a sliver of glass slithering across his forehead.

What next happened was wild and incoherent in all subsequent reports. Shea cared absolutely nothing for results, so long as he got through. When he found his path barred by mounted men, he opened up the throttle wide, shut his eyes, and gripped hard to the wheel. General opinion was that the first bullet had killed him and that the car was running wild; for blood was trickling over his face from his slashed brow, and he was a fearsome sight.

The dust-white flivver smashed head-on into the mass of men and horses. It paused as though for breath, then went ahead. The radiator was boiling over; and when that red-hot projectile began to bore its way, things happened. The steam seared into a big mule, and the mule instantly began to plunge and kick. Two horses went down and the flivver climbed over them and their riders. A vaquero was pitched across the hood and with screams of anguish managed to leap away to earth. A horse sat on the right-hand fender and toppled over upon his rider as the car went ahead.

After a moment Thady Shea opened his eyes and looked back upon a scene of wonderful confusion. Men and horses strewed the ground or were plunging in all directions. With a sigh of relief Thady Shea found that he was still going forward; so, in order to avoid the bullets that came swarming and buzzing after him, he aimed for the nearest cañon, which was not his proper road at all, and followed the trail blindly.

An hour later this trail petered out at an abandoned mine in the bad lands. With a vague general idea of his directions, Shea went plunging off through the sand, winding his way past huge, eroded masses and amid weird pinnacles of wind-blown rock. Somewhere past noon he was in the lava beds, and was apprised of the fact by his tires blowing out one by one.

Lack of pneumatic cushions did not trouble Shea in the least. He punished the poor flivver unmercifully, and by the eternal miracle of flivvers the car kept going. Shea climbed rocky masses, shoved through sand, rolled over jutty fields of volcanic rock, and when the afternoon was half gone, came upon automobile tracks. He had found his road at last. From the tracks, he could tell that the sheriff's automobile had lately gone that way—but in the direction of Silver City.

When, late in the afternoon, Shea came to Number Sixteen, it was deserted. Upon the door of the shack which Mrs. Crump had occupied was pinned a brief note. It read:

Thady: Set rite here till I get back. We are pinched but not for long. My gun is over my bunk. Set tite. Yours,
— M. CRUMP.

Methodically, Shea went to the other shack and began to wash the dried blood from his face, plastering the cut on his brow.

In front of him he propped the note and studied it, tried to read between the lines. It had been written, he thought grimly, as a forlorn hope, a desperate chance that Thady Shea might yet save the day. Mrs. Crump had not been aware of his culpability; or, if she had been aware of it, she had mercifully indulged in no recriminations.

"Well, I'm here," said Shea, then glanced quickly around. The sound of his voice in that solitude was startling.

He felt in no mood for theatricalisms, and that morning he had given vent to none; but now, when he tried to express himself otherwise, homely words failed him. So long had he mantled himself in the braggadocio rhetoric and rounded phrases of The Profession, that he could not rid himself of the bluff which had bolstered up his years of miserable failure. Therefore, he held his peace and tried to face facts squarely. The lesson of primitive silence was another thing that he learned in this strange land.

Now, for the first time, he became aware that he had not come off undamaged that morning. His body was bruised, his face and head were much cut about by hard knuckles. Also, he had not eaten since the previous night, and hunger was beginning to ride him. So he took temporary possession of Mrs. Crump's shack and began to prepare a meal.

The single room of the shack was fairly large, since it had to serve not only as living quarters for Mrs. Crump, but as a dining room for all hands. The walls were rough and bare; like the bunk in the corner, they were formed from hewn timbers, unchinked. Gilbert had knocked together a big mess table; the seats were puncheon stools; in the lean-to adjoining was the kitchen, consisting of a small sheet-iron stove, frying pan, and a kettle. And yet, about this primitive bareness Mrs. Crump had contrived to throw a fragrance of femininity—a rag of curtain to the unglazed window, a faded photograph of the late departed Crump, a battered clock decorated by a scarlet cactus flower, an ancient, white, mended lace counterpane that covered her bunk. And upon the table, a red cloth that was always spick and span. Only a Mrs. Crump would have bothered to bring such tag ends of womanly presence into this bare and rugged spot in the wilderness.

Contemplating these things, Thady Shea sighed; he sighed at thought of Mehitabel Crump, doomed to live in such a place, destitute of all things her woman's heart must have craved. He ceased his sighing, suddenly aware that his bacon was burned.

Thady Shea knew more about prospecting for tungsten than he did about cooking. His coffee was miserable and wretched in spirit. His bacon was brown and hard as wood. Trying to get the beans warmed throughout, he forgot to stir them until unpleasantly reminded of his remissness. However, by the time he had to light the oil lamp in order to see his food, he had managed to make a fair meal, in quantity if not in quality.

Afterward, he filled his pipe and sat in the doorway, staring upon the empurpled masses of the mountains that were piled into the evening sky, and trying to conclude what he must do next.

Mrs. Crump's scribbled mention of her revolver drew a whimsical smile to his lips. He could not remember having fired a revolver in all his life, except with stage blanks; and he had not the slightest intention of learning the art at this time.

He was slightly surprised at his own lack of feeling in regard to the men whom he had hurt. His one uneasiness was lest he be arrested—or, rather, lest someone try to arrest him. He did not intend to leave Number Sixteen until it was safe to do so; until he was certain the place was secure. Therefore, if any officers appeared, a fight must ensue. Consequences did not matter. Thady Shea was quite willing to face any ultimate dispensation of justice so long as he kept Number Sixteen intact for Mrs. Crump.

"I must make up for what I've done," he reflected. "Then I can go. I am a failure, a sodden wreck upon the shoals of self. Once let my reparation be established, and I shall go forth into the world again to seek the dregs of fortune with the bent diviner's rod of Thespian mimicry."

He broke short off, smiling at his own language.

Shea knew inwardly that the old life was gone from him forever. He looked up at the looming mountains and felt a sudden savage joy in himself; a joy that frightened him, so primitive and sweeping was it. He had fought with men—had conquered them! In a measure he was done with all self-recrimination for his weakness and failure. Those were things of the past. He would not be weak again! Remorse fell away from him, and peace came.

The more he thought about arrest, however, the less probable it seemed. Ben Aimes had given him liquor, which was in defiance of law. Shea already knew that Mackintavers et. al. were not desirous of getting into court unless they had an ironclad hold upon the other fellow; this was proven by Mrs. Crump's having "shot up" Dorales with impunity. If the proceedings of the past twenty-four hours were given a public airing, sundry matters might require explanations which would be uncomfortable for Mackintavers.

No, upon that count he was perhaps safe enough; but there would be other counts. They would try to get him—how? No matter. Here was another reason why he must leave Number Sixteen. He must lose himself from those enemies, and he must not involve Mrs. Crump in the mix-up.

Thus deciding, it must be admitted rather vaguely, Thady Shea knocked out his pipe and sought his bunk. He was not so ill pleased with himself, after all; he would yet save Number Sixteen for Mrs. Crump!

The following morning, for the first time in the weeks since Mrs. Crump had picked him up, Thady Shea relaxed in blissful indolence. He had no idea of how the vein or veins of strontianite should be worked. There was little to do about the cabin. So he climbed the long hogback and settled down to smoke and watch the road that wound down from the cañon toward the lava beds, the road that led into the world.

The day passed idly and uneventful. With its passing, Shea felt more assured that his theory was correct; that he was not to be arrested. So convinced of this was he, that when, toward sunset, he discerned a dusty streak betokening the approach of an automobile, he made certain that Mrs. Crump was returning.

Thady Shea sat where he was, resolved to tell her frankly the whole story of his disgrace, then to pause for no argument, but to go. He did not so misjudge her as to think that she would kick him out; still, he felt that he had been false to her trust, and as a part of his penance he must go away, until he might be able to come back a man renewed. A most indistinct idea, this, but strongly persistent. Besides, he would now be a marked man and he must not involve her in his possible danger.

Somewhat to his surprise and uneasiness, as the approaching flivver drew up the cañon Shea could not recognize the gigantic figure of Mehitabel Crump aboard. He saw only three men in the car, and he knew none of them. Two in the rear seat were evidently natives; from the dirty and heavily laden appearance of the car, Shea deduced that these men had come upon no errand of the law. They seemed, rather, to be prospectors or campers.

Near the dust-white flivver the car came to a halt. The driver alighted, and having previously made out the motionless figure of Thady Shea on the hillside above, waved a hand and started upward. The two natives climbed out and began to unstrap bundles.

As the visitor came near to him, Shea saw that the man was powerfully built, roughly dressed, and possessed striking gray eyes beneath black brows and hair.

"Howdy, old-timer!" greeted the new arrival, pausing with outstretched hand and a frank smile. "My name's Logan, Tom Logan. We got lost over in the lava beds and struck your auto tracks. We're prospecting. You don't mind if we camp out here for the night?"

Shea rose and gravely shook hands.

"Not a bit, my friends," he said, then pointed a hundred yards beyond the halted car. "You see that big rock down the valley? Instruct your comrades to make camp at that point or below it."

Logan gave him a puzzled look. That word "valley" was strange in these parts.

"Eh, partner? You're not joking?"

"Sir, the habiliments of jest do not become me," returned Shea, his cavernous eyes piercingly steady.

"But this is all free country, isn't it?"

"It is not. No person may intrude upon this property, sir. You are welcome to water and food if your needs be such, and I am fain of your company. Kindly instruct your knaves to move as I have said."

For a moment Logan met the gravely firm gaze of Shea, then turned and lifted his hands to his mouth. He shouted something

in the patois, to which the two natives waved assent. They turned
their car and took it to the rock that marked the limit of Mrs.
Crump's location in the cañon. Logan began to roll a cigarette
with deft fingers.

"Prospecting hereabouts, I presume?" he inquired. "I didn't
get your name."

Shea found himself warming to the cultivated accents.

"My name, sir, is Shea."

"W-whew!" A long whistle broke from Logan, whose thin
lips parted in a smile. "So you're the man! I heard about you at
Zacaton City last night. They say you cleaned up Aimes and
his crowd for giving you a drink, and that you threatened to do
worse to any man who offered you one again! Good thing I
didn't do it, eh? Glad to meet you, Shea. I'm set against liquor
myself. You've sure become famous in this part of the country!"

Thady Shea did not altogether like the swarthy features and
the odd contrast between steely eyes and coarse black hair, but
he did like applause. He took the stranger down to the shacks
and when Logan set about cooking an excellent dinner, Shea
was delighted.

Over their meal the two men conversed at length, chiefly on
the subject of mining. Tom Logan asked no questions about
Number Sixteen, but he formed the private opinion that Thady
Shea was earnest, upright, and a simpleton. Two thirds of this
diagnosis was correct. The other third was destined to make
trouble for Tom Logan.

At last, over their third pipe, Logan yawned.

"This here is a queer country," he observed. "You're prospecting for gold hereabouts, of course. But d'you know, Shea, the
old prospecting business is changed? Yes, it is. Nowadays two
thirds of the prospectors turn up their noses at gold. There are
new things in the field, things that pay better than gold.

"Platinum, for instance; or tungsten or manganese. Take my
own case—I'm one of a dozen men sent out by a big New York
chemical house. I'm after strontium. It comes in two forms,

celestite and strontianite. Celestite brings about twenty dollars a ton at seaboard; but strontianite, when converted into nitrates, brings five hundred. The average old-time prospector hasn't the chemical knowledge to find such things as those."

"Maybe," said Shea, reflectively. "But yonder hillock, black against the stars, holds in its deep heart veins of mineral; and in those veins, my friend, there runs an ichor bearing the self-same name as that you seek."

Logan stared over this for a moment. Then:

"By jasper! D'you mean that you've got strontianite here?"

"So they do tell me," averred Shea, modestly. He added with frankness, that while he held a third interest in the claim, he knew little of minerals.

Logan displayed a cordial and friendly interest, and asked to see samples. Shea found one or two and set them forth, telling what he knew of the veins. The interest of the visitor grew and waxed enthusiastic. Logan examined the samples closely, and then his gray eyes suddenly struck up at Shea.

"Look here!" he exclaimed, eagerly. "Would you, provided the veins and so forth run as you describe them, accept ten thousand dollars cash for your interest in this location?"

To Thady Shea this offer came like a thunderbolt from a clear sky.

"You see," pursued Logan, "a deposit like this would answer my company's purposes admirably. We might never find another like it. Ten thousand is not a large offer, but it would be a year or more before you'd begin to pull money out of the property. Say yes, and I'll examine the location to-morrow; if it's what you say, I'll buy your right and interest in the property, sign the papers, and before to-morrow night you'll cash my check."

Shea rose to his feet. He wanted to get away from the influence of this man's personality. He wanted to ask counsel from the friendly stars.

"I'll think it over," he said, unsteadily. "By myself—"

"Sure," Logan agreed, heartily. "I'll make out the papers, eh? We're not the kind of men to haggle and fight each other for price."

Thady Shea stalked forth into the darkness, his soul a riot of emotions. "Ten thousand dollars!" he murmured, staring up at the blazing stars. What a sum to turn over to Mrs. Crump upon leaving! With that sum, Mrs. Crump could at once begin development work, independently of Logan's company. With that sum, she could set trucks at work hauling ore to the railroad. With that sum, she could do—anything!

It never occurred to him that he might keep the money for himself; it never occurred to him that he was actually one third owner of the mine, and could sell out any time. Never had he thought about money in connection with Number Sixteen; he had not mentally placed his partnership with Mrs. Crump upon any financial basis. It was because of this very simplicity of thought that Mrs. Crump had felt drawn to him. It was because of this, too, that she had instructed Coravel Tio to record the entire property in the name of Thady Shea, in order to camouflage her ownership from the many eyes of Sandy Mackintavers. But this Shea did not know.

Thady Shea came to the big gray bowlder that marked the limit of the cañon location. He stood against it, gazing upward at the stars, lost in his dream. The rocky mass shut off from him the flickering fire, built by Logan's native companions. Behind, the light in the shack was as another star. He was alone. He was alone, and in the valley of decision.

Ten thousand dollars—for Mrs. Crump! Never had Thady Shea visioned so much money all in one lump. Nor did he now vision it as his own.

Shea did not know that he was technically and legally the owner of Number Sixteen. But the fact was on record, and Tom Logan knew it perfectly well. Back in the shack, under the oil lamp, Logan was already chuckling over the cleverly drawn papers which would make him the sole owner of Number

Sixteen—for the comparatively unimportant sum of ten thousand dollars! He had persuaded Sandy Mackintavers to gamble that sum, to play it as a table stake.

CHAPTER VIII

DORALES GOES TO TOWN

STANDING BY that big bowlder, Shea suddenly awakened from his dream. Out of the night on the other side of the bowlder, where the dim fire of the two natives had flickered into red embers, floated a slow, musical laugh and a few words. The patois was totally unknown to Shea. One of those words, however, drifted across the darkness and smote upon his brain with jarring force. The laugh, too, was not honest; it was a silky laugh, a laugh pregnant with sly meanings and furtive humours. The word was "Dorales."

Shea trembled. Dorales! Why did these natives speak of Dorales in this way?

Now it came into his mind how Tom Logan had known all about him; how Logan had been in Zacaton City the previous night; how Logan had gotten lost in the lava beds—even to Shea's innocence a very improbable thing. Prospectors for limestone formations do not enter the lava beds.

Latent suspicion crystallized within Shea's brain. Tom Logan was no other than Abel Dorales; he was certain of it, he knew it absolutely. His eyes were opened, and he sought for no proof.

Dorales had intended to come here, thinking the place deserted. In Zacaton City he had learned that Thady Shea was probably at Number Sixteen. He had come with cunning intent, he had come with cunning words and a false tongue. The offer of ten thousand dollars might or might not be genuine; no matter!

To the terribly childlike Shea it seemed that Providence had sent that low word and laugh through the night to his ears, to save him from temptation. At thought of how, a few minutes ago, he had been on the point of swallowing the gilded lure of Dorales, he shivered and wiped sweat from his brow.

He turned about and started toward the shacks.

Beside the table where the oil lamp burned, Dorales was sitting and writing. He filled out a previously prepared paper which would transfer to the Empire State Chemical Company, for the sum of ten thousand dollars, all the rights, holdings, and so forth, of Thaddeus Shea in the property underfoot. The company in question consisted of Sandy Mackintavers.

This paper ready for signatures and witnessing, Dorales produced a blank check which bore the almost illegible but widely known signature of A. Mackintavers. This Dorales filled out in the name of Thaddeus Shea, and in the amount of ten thousand dollars. At this instant he heard a hoarse voice whisper his name—"Dorales!"

"Well?" He glanced up sharply, taken by surprise.

Into the lighted doorway stepped Thady Shea, his cavernous eyes blazing. For an instant Dorales was too completely astounded to move—astounded by the realization of how he had just betrayed himself, astounded by the fact that this gaunt fellow was no simpleton after all!

That instant of indecision was fatal. Dorales pushed back his chair and came to his feet, one hand sliding to his coat pocket. Too late! The big fingers of Thady Shea gripped down on his wrist, and Shea's right hand took him by the left shoulder, and he was staring into the blazing black eyes of the man he had thought to cheat.

"I am glad to meet you, friend Dorales!" A grim smile sat on Shea's wide lips. "The airy tongues that syllable men's names have borne to me your rightful cognomen."

Dorales writhed under that iron grip. His left hand drove up to Shea's face, landed hard. From his lips broke a shout for aid.

Under the blow, Shea staggered; he knew nothing of fighting. He did know, however, that the shout of Dorales would bring the two Mexicans, and the knowledge fired him. He merely threw himself bodily and blindly at Dorales and carried the latter to the floor.

Luck was kind. Dorales, trying not to fall underneath, writhed aside; the impetus of Shea's rush, or rather fall, threw Abel Dorales headlong against the wall and knocked him senseless.

After a moment Shea realized that Dorales was knocked out, relaxed his iron grip, and rose. His first thought was to turn out the lamp. Then, taking from the corner the axe helve, Shea passed outside the shack. He discerned two figures running toward him in the starlight, and he strode at them.

The two natives were not at all sure of what had been going on. They called to Shea, who made no answer but came steadily at them. Hesitant, they awaited his approach, again addressing him in English. For response, Shea heaved up the axe helve and struck the nearer man senseless.

Here was answer enough. The second man whipped up a ready revolver and fired hastily; too hastily, for the bullet only whipped Shea's lean cheek and passed over the hogback. An instant later the axe helve broke the man's arm.

"Be quiet!" commanded Shea; then considered that the groaning wretch could not well obey such an order with a smashed arm. "Go down and climb into your automobile. Wait there."

"Si, señor." The native turned and went into the night, groaning.

Stooping, Shea picked up the body of the second man, the one whom he had stricken senseless. He heaved it up over his shoulder, and returned to the shack. There he lighted a match, got the lamp burning again, and clumsily tied Abel Dorales hand and foot. He rightly considered that the fight was taken out of the two natives.

Dorales evinced no symptoms of recovery. Shea threw some water over the face of his native prisoner, and presently the man sat up and stared around. At sight of Shea's figure, he shrank back and crossed himself.

"I'll not hurt you," said Shea. "Where's Mackintavers?"

"At the ranch, señor," whimpered the wide-eyed native.

"Is he coming here?"

"No, señor, not until Señor Dorales sends for him."

"That will not be for some time." And Shea smiled. "Do you know where Mrs. Crump is?"

"I heard Señor Dorales say that she would not get there until to-morrow night, señor."

This explained to Shea why Dorales had planned on cleaning up the sale so hastily. It also set his mind at rest about Mackintavers, whose arrival he had feared.

There was no doubt whatever that Dorales had figured things closely and accurately. Therefore, Mrs. Crump would return upon the following afternoon or evening, and in the meantime no other attempt would be made upon the property.

With this thought in mind, Thady Shea set about making his departure, for he intended to be gone when Mrs. Crump arrived home. If Dorales were safely out of the way for a day or two, there would be no danger in leaving the mine deserted; and Shea was already possessed of a scheme for putting Dorales in cold storage.

Prompt to act upon the swift impulse in his mind, Shea turned over the cleverly drawn paper which Dorales had been studying, and upon its back wrote a note to Mrs. Crump. The check caught his eye, and he pulled it toward him; smiling sardonically, he read and reread that magic slip of paper which stood for ten thousand dollars.

He picked up the check and held it for a moment over the oil lamp—then he quickly jerked it back.

"No, I'll leave it," he muttered. "She'll know I'm honest, perchance! It will be a tongue most eloquent."

That sardonic smile still curving his wide lips, he turned over the check and carefully indorsed it; across the back of the paper he wrote the same name which he had signed to the note. The whimsical thought came to him that, if he presented this paper at a bank, he would get ten thousand dollars for Mrs. Crump; he had no intention of so presenting it, however—had he not refused the proffered negotiations? He indorsed that check merely as a mute message to Mrs. Crump. It quite escaped him that, by so indorsing it, he had made it good.

He picked up the epistle which he had written, and read it over, frowning:

> MADAM: If you do not already know of my unhappy share in your misfortunes, you may be easily apprised of it from other lips. Farewell! I take my leave to seek an errant soul upon the roads, and I shall not return until some testing has surfeited my most uneasy spirit.
>
> — THADDEUS R. SHEA.

He folded up the note, and nodded to himself.

" 'Tis not so clear as crystal, yet 'twill serve," he murmured.

Whether Mrs. Crump would fully understand the reasons for his departure was immaterial, since Shea himself did not fully understand them; at least, he had not figured them into concrete bases. His idea of doing penance, of seeking either ultimate strength or ultimate failure again in the world, was vague. His secondary motive, that of not drawing his benefactress into his own danger from the Mackintavers forces, was equally vague, since Mrs. Crump was far more imperilled and far better equipped to face such peril than he.

However, it is these vague impulses which often lead men upon the trail of fate, and thus it proved with Thady Shea.

He left the note upon the table, and with it the indorsed check and legally phrased paper, knowing that these would in some measure make matters clear to Mrs. Crump. Then he procured that lady's whiskey and poured a generous portion into a tin cup. This time, he deliberately smelled of it, and smiled grimly. Mrs. Crump kept on hand a vial of laudanum for the sake of recurrent toothache, and from this vial he dropped a little of the drug into the whiskey.

"Friend Dorales will sleep to-night, methinks," he said to the staring native captive. "Lift up his head!"

The native picked up the head and shoulders of the still senseless Dorales. Forcing open the thin, strong lips, Shea poured his mixture into the man's mouth. Dorales choked, but swallowed it and began to revive.

Shea packed his few belongings, regretfully left the historic axe helve for Mrs. Crump, then motioned his prisoner to help him lift Dorales. The latter was now swearing luridly but feebly. Together they carried him out into the darkness.

Ten minutes later Dorales was snoring in the tonneau of Mackintavers' flivver, beside the injured native. By the light of the lamps, the uninjured captive was working under the directions of Shea, who had realized that upon reaching home Mrs. Crump would be unable to use her own car without tires.

So Shea stripped the enemy car, left the tires beside the dust-white flivver, and then climbed into his captured vehicle. Having disarmed his conquered foemen, he had nothing to fear from them, and headed his bumpy equipage toward No Agua. When the cañon road warned him that he was close to that lone hovel of desolation, he stopped the car and took from his pocket Mrs. Crump's flask into which he had emptied the laudanum vial. He turned to the two natives, one of whom was groaning and shivering, the other merely shivering.

"Friends," he said, sonorously, "drink—or take the consequences."

Knowing from the example of Abel Dorales that the flask contained nothing worse than sleep, mingled with liquor, the two natives drank the contents with avidity. Shea tossed away the empty flask, envy in his eye; he wanted a drink very badly—but he did not want one badly enough to take it.

Passing the No Agua store with a rattle and clatter, Shea considered swiftly. If he went south to Silver City he might meet Mrs. Crump, and he had no desire to meet her at present. If he went west, he would get into Arizona. All he knew about Arizona was founded upon the drama of that name; the prospect of being scalped by Apaches or otherwise mutilated did not invite his soul particularly.

So he turned east to Zacaton City, confident that he could pass through that nest of enemies before dawn, and with a vague scheme already in his mind. All he wanted was to get clear away, and he mentally blessed that vial of laudanum.

It was shortly before dawn when the snoring mechanic in Aimes' garage was awakened by a tall, gaunt stranger.

"Friend," said Shea to the yawning mechanic, "in this my vehicle behold three villains, scoundrels of the deepest dye! But yesternight they tried to jump my claim, wherefore I laid them by the heels, and charge you, upon your honest visage, guard them well until the sheriff shall appear to claim them."

After some repetition the astonished mechanic gathered that this gaunt stranger had brought in three claim jumpers to be held until the sheriff arrived. Not having participated in the events of Sunday morning, the mechanic was blissfully ignorant of Shea's identity, and Thady had no intention of disclosing it. Despite protest, Shea left the crippled flivver in the garage, the three snoring occupants being obviously safe for another twenty-four hours. Having been carefully dirtied and disguised by Dorales himself, the flivver was not recognized immediately as that of Sandy Mackintavers.

These things successfully accomplished, Thady Shea faded into the gray dawn. For lack of better direction, he took the

rough and rugged road that led off to Datil and the transcon-
tinental highway into Magdalena. He had no illusions about
arrest not being probable in *this* case, and he desired to avoid
arrest.

Zacaton City was ere long in a roar of half-wrathful enjoyment. The three "claim jumpers," who slept like the dead and
refused to be awakened, were soon known as Abel Dorales, tied
hand and foot, and two natives from the Mackintavers ranch,
one having a broken arm. The garage mechanic's description of
Thady Shea was accurate and recognizable. Details were lacking
and could not be obtained until the drugged men awakened—
but details were largely unnecessary.

Ben Aimes did not telephone to Mackintavers at the ranch;
at the time, this seemed a rather superfluous detail. The news
bearer would have a thankless and possibly dangerous job, so
Ben Aimes left Mackintavers alone, and left Dorales to tell the
sorry tale in person. However, Aimes swore out warrants charg-
ing battery and other things, and sent automobiles forth to
bring in Thady Shea.

Him they did not find; but they went as far as Magdalena,
spreading the story as they progressed. Within three days, this
immediate section of the state was in a roar of laughter; Dorales
had a reputation as "the worst man to monkey with" in existence.
Added to the joke was the story of Thady Shea and the axe
helve, which travelled fast and far. Neither story reached the
Mackintavers ranch fast enough, however.

On the afternoon following Thady Shea's desertion of
Number Sixteen, Mrs. Crump arrived there in a hired car from
Silver City. She came alone; Gilbert and Lewis were in jail
awaiting bail, and she came only to make sure that Number
Sixteen had escaped the ravishers.

By this time Mrs. Crump knew all about what had happened
to Thady Shea in Zacaton City, and how the disaster had come
upon her, but she had made no comments. At the shack, she
found the papers which Thady Shea had left. She read his note,

and muttered something about "damned fool." Then she took the check which he had indorsed, returned to her hired car, and before midnight was back in Silver City.

At nine the next morning the Silver City bank telephoned Sandy Mackintavers over long distance regarding a check for ten thousand dollars issued to one Thady Shea, and properly indorsed, which had been presented for payment by Mrs. Crump. Promptly and delightedly Mackintavers gave it his O. K. Quite naturally, he considered that Abel Dorales had carried his mission to success, and that Number Sixteen now belonged to the Empire State Chemical Company.

But that evening, when Dorales arrived with new tires on the flivver, Mackintavers learned what had really taken place. Then he telephoned to Silver City in all haste, only to find that he was out ten thousand big round dollars. He had gambled, and he had lost his stake.

Dorales spent a most unpleasant evening. Despite everything, even the monetary loss, which rankled to the very bottom of his soul, Mackintavers had a deep grain of humour. This was the first time he had ever known Abel Dorales to be put absolutely down and out; he gave his humour full vent until Dorales, who had no humour whatever, writhed under the lash.

"It's your loss most of all," growled Dorales, white lipped and venomous.

"Aiblins, yes." Mackintavers fell grave. "We'll leave Mrs. Crump alone for the present; never fear, I'll get that money back, with interest! I've a scheme in the back of my head that will work on her a bit later. Are ye going to hide out till the laughing's done with?"

"Hide—hell!" snarled Dorales, viciously. "The first man that laughs to my face, except you, gets something to remember. And," he added, slowly, "I'm not so sure about excepting you, Sandy."

"There, there, cannot ye take a joke?" returned Mackintavers, hastily. "I've suffered the most, but leave Mrs. Crump be for the present. I want to get the matter o' those stone idols settled, and under cover o' the noise it will make when I become a scientist, then we'll take over this strontianite mine.

"I want ye to go up to Santa Fé, and get a big sack o' silver dollars. I've me eye on two or three o' them Cochiti redskins and I think ye can bribe 'em. If—"

"What about this man Shea?" snapped Dorales. "I'm going to get him if it takes me ten years! I'm going to write my name in his hide with a knife!"

"Ye shall; he'll be here when ye get back from Santa Fé," soothed Mackintavers. "He can't hide out long, Abel. I'll have him held for ye."

"You'd better," said the other, sourly. "I don't like wasting time on these idols, anyway. I never knew any good to come of bothering the Indian gods, Sandy."

Mackintavers only laughed, although not without a frown to follow the laugh. He was wondering if the presence of those gods in his house had brought him the loss of ten thousand dollars. He was the last man on earth to let superstition alter his plans; yet he was Scottish, and he could not help wondering—just a little.

CHAPTER IX

THE WICKER DEMIJOHN

AS HAS been related, Thady Shea somewhat vaguely set out upon the way to Magdalena, after disposing of his shoeless flivver and its snoring load.

The dawn came up and found him plodding onward. An hour later he was hailed from the roadside by a venerable ancient having one very blue eye and a long white beard. This worthy proved to be a tramp printer, who intended to get work at Magdalena when his money gave out.

For the present, however, the ancient had no intention of working; so he proposed a road partnership, stating that he liked Shea's looks. Thady Shea wanted to sleep, which "Dad" Griffith, as the ancient was named, deemed a highly laudable ambition.

Accordingly, a little while afterward, Shea found himself snugly ensconced in a camp well back from the road and well hidden in a clump of trees. Before sleeping, he explored his pockets and found some money, left from the sum given him by Mrs. Crump for his Zacaton City purchases.

"Take it, friend," he said, drowsily, thrusting the money upon the ancient. "Take it, and add it to thy scanty store, that so we may have wherewithal to live."

"You bet I will, partner," and Dad Griffith seized it. "It'll keep us quite a spell, with what I got. No sense workin', I says, when they's no need. I figger on gettin' a job to Magdalena when I got to work. I had a job there two year ago. These here goshly-gorful linotypes is puttin' honest printers out o' business. Why, I seen th' day—"

In the midst of a dissertation upon the elegancies of hand-set type and the blasted frightfulness of an existence surrounded by linotype machines, Shea stretched out and fell asleep. The ancient droned along, regardless. When Shea wakened toward sunset, old Griffith was still discoursing upon the same topic.

Over a tiny smokeless fire Griffith conjured biscuits, coffee, and beans, and the two men ate. Thady Shea probed his companion's mind for future plans, and found only a vague emptiness; the ancient liked to spend each night in a different spot, that was all. Thady Shea proposed, with pursuit in mind, that it might be better to camp during the day and to tramp at night.

At this suggestion the ancient winked his one intensely blue eye. He winked with the uncanny gusto of an old man, with the horrible craftiness of an old man. His one eye winked, and the ancient was transformed. He became an emblem of doddering truancy, a living symbol of the soul which desires ever to flee responsibilities and to shirk the onus of labour inherited from Father Adam.

"Suits me, pardner. I used to do that over in Missouri, one time, 'count of a hawg bein' missed from a pen. Anyhow, these nights is too cold to sleep 'thout blankets, which mine ain't extra good.

"Still, a spry young feller like you, Thady, ought to have more get up an' get to him than to be gettin' in a mess o' trouble. Take a goshly-gorful old ranger like me, and it's all right; I'm a sinful man, an' proud of it. But you, now—you'd ought to be aimin' for something. I know, I do! That's the trouble with folks; ain't got no aim ahead. But no use talkin'. You got your reasons, I reckon."

Thady Shea sat and stared into the fire. He did not take the hint to retail his story. He was suddenly thinking.

Memory worked within him. "It ain't lack of ambition that makes folks mis'able and unsatisfied; it's lack o' purpose!" Mrs. Crump had said those words, and they had been burned into Shea's brain. Purpose, indeed! What purpose now lay ahead, except the vague desire to rehabilitate himself? To become a vagrant with this tramp printer—why, this would be to shake off all the shackles of purpose! Yet, what else was there to do? What could be done, except to evade the law which by this time must be seeking him?

His head drooped. Was some higher Power extending its hand against him, closing every avenue of escape from his old drifting existence, forcing him back into vagrancy? His eyes widened under the thought. The thought staggered him. Then, slowly, his mouth tightened, his wide lips drew firmly clenched. A flush of fever darkened his high cheekbones.

Very well; he would go on fighting! For once the superstitious nature of the man was borne down by his inward anger, was borne down by the impotent feeling that he was a pawn in Destiny's game; he rebelled against it. He rebelled against everything.

"By heaven, I'll *make* a purpose!" he mentally vowed. "I'll look for one—find one—fight for one!"

Even as the words rose in him, he choked down a vague feeling that they were false and erroneous, a feeling that this purpose could not be sought, but must seek him out, must come to him of itself. Yet he choked down the feeling, repulsed it. He reiterated his mental vow, fiercely insistent upon it.

All this while the ancient had been droning something about the beauties of the old flat-bed presses, and the goshly-gorfulness of machine printing. Now Shea became aware of a more personal note in the droning.

"If I was you," and the ancient chuckled in his dirty white beard, transfixing Thady Shea with his one bright-blue eye, "if I was you, I'd grow whiskers!

"They's places and places I can't never go no more without these here whiskers. Yes, they is! I'm a sinful man an' proud of it; mebbe ye think I'm old, but I can show you young fellers a thing or two, he, he! Grow whiskers, Thady. You can take 'em with ye to go a-sinning, and then go back over the same trail without 'em, and nobody the wiser!"

Shea's gorge rose. He suddenly saw Dad Griffith as the latter really was—a foul old man, a worthless wastrel of humanity, seemingly dead to all higher things. He grew afraid for himself; he was vaguely alarmed, as though he had touched some slimy, crawling thing in the darkness. He came to his feet with an impellent desire to crush this unholy man like a toad, to flee into the night, to lie under the stars and seek clearance for his troubles. However, he did none of these things. Shea reached for his pipe, filled it, lighted it with an ember from the fire. Here he got a new sensation—the tang and sweetness of an ember-lighted pipe!

"Let's be moving," said Thady Shea, crisply. "It's a fine night."

An hour later they were plodding along, sharing the load of provisions. Thady Shea was quite aware that something was wrong with him in the body, but he felt no definite pain. It was an errant "something" which he could not place, and which he was too uplifted in spirit to heed.

The night wore on. With every step, Thady Shea was learning from the lore of Dad Griffith. He was learning the worldly wise lore of the roads—to walk with straight feet, to carry his body uphill on bended knees, to take the high side of a wet trail. The ancient talked continually, eternally. The ancient seemed to like Thady Shea immensely.

Some time after midnight they left the road by a faint and unknown trail, followed it until they were weary, and then camped. Griffith had a pair of tattered blankets. Thady Shea refused to share them; he slept in his clothes. When he wakened at sunrise his head was heavy with fever. A mile distant the ancient descried a creek, and they moved over to it for the day. Thady Shea felt peculiar, and detailed his symptoms, whereupon the ancient produced a tattered little case of leather. He opened the case and disclosed three vials.

"All the med'cine a man needs, I claim," he declared. "Middle one's quinine; right's physic; left's physic again, only more so. Take your choice, one or all!"

"Give me the more so," said Thady, who felt miserable in the extreme.

The ancient began to look alarmed. His one intensely blue eye shone with an uneasy light. His continual talk became querulous. After a time he forced Thady Shea to continue their progress; the trail, said he, must lead them to a ranch. Groaning, Shea protested; but presently he yielded to the urgings of Griffith. The two men followed the trail.

There was a man named Fred Ross, who had homesteaded a cañon in the hills beyond the Datils. Thus far unmarried, although he had his hopes, he lived alone; a hard, rough man, kindly at heart, redly wrinkled of face, and keenly alert of eye, he shot beaver and turkey when the forest rangers were not around, and fared well. Indeed, he was wont to say that he was the last man in the United States to know the taste of that succulent morsel, a beaver's tail.

Fred Ross was plowing on the flat behind his shack when he observed the approach of a tattered old man who moved in trembling haste. Having no liking for tramps, Ross set his hands on his hips and met the visitor with a vigilant eye.

"Well?" he snapped. "Who in time are *you?*"

"Don't matter 'bout me, mister," said the other, agitatedly pawing a long and dirty white beard. "A friend o' mine is down the cañon a ways, plumb petered out. He was took sick last night—I reckon he's got a touch o' fever. D'you s'pose you could let him lay somewheres—mebbe in that cowshed yonder?"

"You be damned, you old fool," said Ross, harshly. "I ain't got no room for sick men in my shed—which ain't no cowshed, neither. Where is he?"

"He—he give out by them trees," faltered Dad Griffith, backing away. "I got a little money, mister—"

"You be blistered, you an' your money!" roared Ross. "I don't want no tramps around here, savvy? I got trouble of my own. Let's have a look at this friend o' yours—if you-all are tryin' any skin game on *me*, look out!"

He strode forward, and Dad Griffith fluttered away. After him strode Ross. Ten minutes later they came to the gaunt figure of Thady Shea lying beneath some scrub oaks and muttering faintly. Ross leaned over him then straightened up and faced the ancient.

"You—on your way!" he said, roughly, "I'll take care o' this feller, but I don't aim to keep two of ye."

"Devil take ye, I don't want none of ye!" quavered Griffith in querulous anger. "I'm goin' to Magdalena to get me a job; you tell him so when he can travel, ye goshly-gorful old ranch hand!"

Disdaining a response, Ross stooped; after some effort, he got Thady Shea in the "fireman's grip" and staggered erect, the delirious man still muttering. He turned and walked toward his shack, striding heavily under the burden. Dad Griffith hesitated, then wagged his beard—he did not deem it wise to follow.

"Hey!" he lifted his voice after the departing rancher. "You be good to him, hear me? Mind my words, if ye ain't good to him I'll—I'll come back and burn ye out some night!"

Ross paid no heed but strode on out of sight. Dad Griffith shook his fist in senile rage, then slowly, and with a sigh, turned about and started in the opposite direction.

The shack which Ross had built, anticipating matrimony, was a two-room affair with a lean-to kitchen. Grunting beneath his load, Ross stooped into the house and deposited Thady Shea upon an iron bed.

Ross came erect, panting, and stared down at Shea's fever-flushed features. He scratched his head, as though in perplexity, and his eyes were suddenly very kindly.

"Poor devil!" he said, being a man who talked much to himself. "Poor devil! Got a real good face, too. What in time can I do? The car's broke down and there's no doctor closer'n Magdalena anyhow. Well, I never knowed whiskey to fail curin' any trouble, and I guess a bit o' quinine will help out. Thank the Lord I got whiskey to burn!"

He went to a cupboard in the corner and drew forth a wicker demijohn, a new demijohn, a demijohn that hung heavy in his hand. Upon the chair beside the bed he put a big crockery cup, thick and heavy. He poured whiskey into it; he filled it nearly to the brim with raw red liquor; a ray of sunlight fell upon the cup and made it seem filled with rich thin blood.

"Just for a starter," murmured Ross. "Now the quinine."

The hours passed, and darkness fell. Ross went out to stable and bed down his team. He came back, ate, resumed his vigil.

Ross was starkly amazed by his muttering patient. Cup upon cup of whiskey and quinine he poured down the gaunt man's throat; the man drank it like water, avidly, without visible effect. He seemed to soak up the raw red liquid as a sponge soaks up water. It seeped down his throat and was gone.

"My Lord!" exclaimed Ross at last, awed despite himself. "The man ain't human!"

Thady Shea was human; although invisible, the effect was there. Through the hours of darkness his sonorous voice rose and filled the shack. He spoke of things past the understanding of the watching Ross. He used strange names—names like Ophelia or Rosalind or Desdemona; at times passion shook his voice, a fury of resonant passion; at times his words trembled with grief, his rolling words quavered and surged with a vehemently agonized utterance, until the listening Ross felt a vague ache wrenched into his own throat.

About midnight, Thady Shea fell asleep. It was a deep, full slumber, a slumber of stertorous breathing, a sound and absolute slumber, a drunken slumber. Thady Shea lay motionless except for his deeply heaving chest. His hands, face, and body were glistening wet, were wet with perspiration that streamed from him, were wet with salty sweat oozing from his fever-baked flesh. Fred Ross turned out the lamp and climbed into a bunk in the corner.

"That ends it," he said, drowsily. "He'll sweat out the fever and sleep off the whiskey, and wake up cured. Can't beat whiskey! Cures everything!"

Upon the following morning Ross returned from his chores to find Thady Shea still lustily snoring, the fever gone. He got breakfast and departed to his work, leaving the coffee ready to hand. From time to time he came in from the nearer end of the flat to inspect his patient. He was a big man, a rough-tongued man, a deep-hearted man.

Thady Shea wakened to an uncomfortable sensation. He dimly and vaguely recognized the sensation; he was bewildered and frightened by it. He had felt that uncomfortable sensation many times in his life, always on the morning after a night spent with the jorum.

He tried to sit up, and succeeded, only to close his eyes before a blinding wave of pain. A headache? It went with the other symptoms, of course. He had no remembrance of drinking. Indeed, he had a fierce remembrance of having meant never to drink again. Where was he and how had he come here? His last memory was of trees, and the ancient helping him as he sank down. He looked around; the strange room bewildered him.

He was maddeningly conscious that his body, his soul, his whole being, was a soaked and impregnated thing, soaked and impregnated with whiskey. His body cried out for more whiskey, his soul writhed within him for more whiskey. His haggard gaze fell upon a cup, on a chair at his bedside. He reached out and picked up the cup. It was half full of bitter whiskey, and a bottle of powdered quinine explained the bitterness.

Even then, Shea hesitated. He hesitated, but he could not resist. No living man could have resisted the fearful outcry of body and soul upon such an awakening. It was no mere craving. It was a tumultuous, riotous, lawless eagerness—a fierceness for whiskey, an awful tormenting passion for whiskey such as he had never before known. That was because of the flood that had seeped and soaked through his whole being. The raw red liquor like thin blood had permeated all his body tissues and nerves, as water permeates the sun-dried earth, leaving it not the hard white earth but the brown soft mud. The earth dries again and cracks open, calling avidly for more water. So with Thady Shea's body and soul.

He drank gulpingly, until the cup was empty. He sat down the cup; it was a heavy cup of thick crockery. His nostrils quivered to the smell of coffee. He began to take in his surroundings, to realize them, to appraise them. He began to understand that he must have been drunk. Drunk! Who was responsible?

A shadow darkened the morning sunlight in the doorway. There on the threshold, a black blotch against the brightness outside, stood Fred Ross, staring at the man who sat on the edge of the bed and stared back at him. Shea saw only a man— the man responsible.

"Did you—" He paused, licked his lips, and continued thickly. "Did you give me whiskey? Did you?"

Ross stepped into the room.

"Yes, I did," he began, roughly. He did not finish.

Something shot from the bedside, something large and thick, something white and heavy, that left the hand of Thady Shea like a bullet. It was the thick, heavy crockery cup. Shea flung it blindly. It struck Ross over the ear with a *"whick!"*

Fred Ross looked vaguely surprised. His knees appeared to give way beneath him. He caught at the table and seemed to swing himself forward, half around. He fell, and lay without moving. The heavy white crockery cup, unhurt by the impact, rolled in the doorway.

Relaxing on the edge of the bed, Thady Shea gave no more attention to Fred Ross, but lowered his face in his two hands. They were big, strong hands; they clutched into his hair and skin until their knuckles stood out white. Shea sat motionless, thus, as though he were trying to produce some exterior which would quell the anguish within him.

His voice rang with a sonorous bitterness as he spoke aloud. The recumbent Ross moved, then sat up with a lithe, agile motion; but Thady Shea did not stir. He was lost in the words that seemed wrung from his very soul.

"I've tried, I've tried! How have I been weak, how have I failed? Yet I have failed. I've been drunk. I always fail."

His speech was heavy, slow, words coming tenuously to his numbed brain. He did not hear the slight sound made by Ross in rising erect, in stepping to the wall. He did not see Ross at all, nor the hand of Ross that plucked a revolver from a holster suspended on the wall. He spoke again, the words coming with more coherence.

"Always an unseen hand blocks me. Is it your doing, oh, God? Before, it was my own fault, for I was weak. This time it was not my fault; I knew nothing about it. God, are You trying to turn me back into the old shiftless life, into the old vagabond, aimless existence? God, are You trying to make me a drunkard again? Are You trying to rob me of all purpose?"

He paused. The breath came from his lungs; it was a deep and uneven breath, a sobbing breath, the breath of one who is fast in the grip of terrible emotion. At him stood and stared Ross. Inch by inch the revolver lowered. The keen, alert, battling eyes of the rancher were filled with perplexity, with comprehension, with a strange gentleness. Again Shea spoke, his face still in his hands:

"I've done my best, God knows! I've put whiskey out of my life, stifled the craving for it, forgotten about it. And now—now! Why is it that even this one purpose is denied me? Is there no help—is there no help? Is there no help for—"

His fingers clenched upon his iron-gray hair, swept through it. His head came up. His blazing black eyes stared into the gaze of Ross. For half a moment the two men looked at each other, motionless.

Then, abruptly, Ross pushed home the revolver into its holster.

"Pardner," he said, casually, "let's have a cup o' coffee."

He went to the stove in the kitchen, raked up charred black brands, opened the draft, and put the coffeepot over the kindling embers. He set two thick crockery cups upon the boards of the table. He got out spoons and sugar and "canned cow." Then he turned to the other room and with a jerk of the head invited his guest.

Thady Shea rose, very unsteadily, and came.

CHAPTER X

MRS. CRUMP SAYS SOMETHING

OVER THE rough table Fred Ross delivered himself. "Something about you I like, Thady Shea," he said, level-eyed. "The old man who fetched you here told me your name. Don't know anything more about you. Didn't know whiskey was bad for you; anyway, it cured the fever. First I knew about you was in yonder, when you talked. Damn good thing for you, pardner! Savvy? Yes.

"Tell you somethin'. I used to be range rider—a puncher, savvy? Forty a month. No future. Never mind the details, but it come to me that if I didn't get somethin' to work for, I might's well quit livin'. So I took up this here quarter section and started in. It cost me dear, I'm tellin' you!

"I sweat blood over every inch o' this here land. Folks said it was no good. I put up this shack, put it up right. I set in to raise crops. I put my body into it. I put my heart into it. I put my livin' eternal soul into it—and by the Lord I'm goin' to win! I had somethin' to work for, that's all."

Ross leaned back. The flame died from his eyes. He surveyed Thady Shea critically, appraisingly, generously.

"When I heard what you said, in yonder," he pursued, "I seen all of a sudden that you were a man like me. Savvy? Yes. I don't blame you, now, for lamming me over the ear like you done. My Lord! Ain't I talked to God like you done in there? Ain't things come up to rip the very guts out o' my soul? Well, it's like that with all folks, I guess, only it comes different. Savvy? Yes. I gave you whiskey, and I was a damn fool. That's all."

Ross rose and began to clatter dishes into the dishpan. Thady Shea rose and went to the doorway. He stood there, looking up the east-running cañon toward the morning sun. He did not see the half-plowed flat, he did not see the horses and plow; he

did not see the piñon trees and the trickle of water. Tears were
in his eyes. For one blazing moment he had seen into the soul
of Fred Ross, the iron soul, the gentle soul, the brave soul of
Fred Ross.

Suddenly he turned about, feeling upon his shoulder the
hand of the other man.

"Shea, you asked a while ago if there wasn't no help. Well,
maybe there is—if you want it. Do you?"

"Yes," said Thady Shea, huskily.

Upon the following morning he started in to work; he was
a bit weak, but he insisted upon working. He dared not do
without working. He began to clear another flat farther up the
cañon, ridding it of brush and scrub oak and piñons.

As he worked, Thady Shea thought much of that wicker
demijohn, back in the cupboard of the shack. Once, when he
came in to luncheon ahead of Ross, he opened the cupboard.
He looked at the clean wicker demijohn, the new demijohn,
the demijohn which hung so heavily and lovingly to the hand;
as he looked, a sunbeam struck the glass behind the woven
wicker and made it seem filled with rich thin blood. Thady Shea
shivered—and shut the door. But he could not shut that demijohn from his thoughts.

He prayed, every hour he worked, that Ross would hide away
that demijohn. He said nothing to Ross about it; he felt vaguely
ashamed to let Ross know of his struggles with himself. He
shrank from revealing how he was tempted.

Days passed. Twice, now, Thady Shea had come in from work
merely to open that door and look at the demijohn. The first
time, he had forced himself to be content with the look. The
second time he hefted it; then he reached for the cork, trembling—but just then the step of Ross approached, and Shea
replaced the demijohn. He knew that he had been saturated
with liquor, that in his involuntary carouse his body had seeped
up the whiskey as the thirsty earth seeps up water. The craving
was there, the wicked craving of the cracked earth for water.

Terrible were the first few nights. Despite weariness, sleep would not come. On tiptoe Thady Shea would sneak out of the shack, out into the bitter cold night, out under the white, cold stars. He would stride up and down the cold earth until the chill ate into his bones; then, shivering, he would tiptoe back and roll up in his blankets, thinking how a drink would warm him.

As the days passed, he worked harder. He slaved until, at darkness, he would nod over his pipe. He did not shave, re-membering the words of the ancient, and his gaunt face became filled and strengthened by an iron-gray beard.

All the while he cursed his aimlessness, his lack of purpose. He was looking out, beyond the present; he was looking over the horizon. He was thinking of Mrs. Crump. He prayed under a sweat-soaked brow that some great flaming purpose would come into his life. The word "purpose" had become to him a creed, a mania.

He did not realize, except very dimly, that for him life had already centred upon one immediate and tremendous purpose: to avoid, to shrink from, that clean wicker demijohn in the corner cupboard! Unawares, the purpose had come to him.

And then, upon a day, Fred Ross patched the broken flivver and went to Datil for grub. Thady Shea was left alone, alone with the ranch, alone with the piñon trees and the horses, alone with the shack, alone with the corner cupboard and the clean wicker demijohn. Fred Ross did not seem to perceive any danger in leaving Shea thus alone.

Fred Ross reached the store at Datil about noon, after a long pull. Datil lay on the highway, where lordly Packards and lowly Fords wended east and west, between California and St Louis. Datil was nothing more than a frame store-hotel-post office. In the rear of the long building were sheds, relics of the days when the far ranchers came in on horseback, of the days when burros and bearded prospectors and unrestricted Indians roused talk of great and blood-stirring events.

A mixed company lunched that day in the long dining room. Ross was too late for the first table, and he stood waiting in the adjoining room, smoking by the huge cobbled fireplace, talking with other men who had drifted along too late for the first serving.

The talk struck upon Thady Shea and the huge joke of which Abel Dorales had been the victim. Ross listened and said nothing, as was his wont. He heard that Thady Shea had skipped the country; had, at any rate, not been found—must have gone over the Arizona line.

"Too bad," commented a sturdy rancher from Quemado way. "He must ha' been a right strapping guy, eh? And what he done down to Zacaton, when Ben Aimes give him a drink—say, ain't ye heard 'bout that? It's sure rich!"

The speaker recounted, with many added elaborations and details, the story of Thady Shea and his axe helve. Fred Ross listened in silence. Fred Ross thought of that heavy white crockery cup; reflectively, he rubbed his head above his ear, and grinned to himself. He was not the only one who had suffered for giving Thady Shea a drink, then!

When the talk turned upon reprisals, Fred Ross listened with more attention. Charges had been sworn out against Shea, it appeared; they had been sworn out by that fool Aimes, but had later been withdrawn. Abel Dorales had seen to it that they had been withdrawn. Abel Dorales had come to Magdalena; there he had half killed three drunken miners who had ventured to taunt him, and for the same reason he had taken a blacksnake to a sheepman. Abel Dorales had given out that he, and he alone, intended to deal with Thady Shea whenever the latter was found. It was a personal matter, outside the law. This attitude met with general approval.

"Not so bad!" reflected Fred Ross, as he passed in to his meal. "Not so bad! The law ain't after him, anyhow. Now, if he's let that demijohn alone to-day, I reckon he's all right. Pretty tough on him, maybe, to leave him alone, but—"

The ins and outs of the business transaction attempted by Dorales, the transaction concerning Number Sixteen, had, of course, not been made public. But the general gist of the matter was an open secret. The joke on Dorales was huge, and was immensely appreciated.

The meal over, Ross went out to his car in order to get his tobacco. He idly observed that alongside his own flivver had been run another, a dust-white flivver with new tires. He paid no attention to it until he was drawn by the sound of a voice which he instantly recognized. He stood quiet, listening, looking toward the two figures on the far side of the dust-white flivver; they did not see him at all.

"No'm," said the voice which Ross had recognized. "No'm, I couldn't get no work to Magdalena. Things is in a goshly-gorful state in the printing business! I done walked here, aiming to make for Saint Johns, over the Arizony line. Seein's you're headed that way, ma'am, if ye could give me a lift—"

"Walked here, did ye?" cut in a voice strange to Ross. "Had any vittles?"

"Not to speak of, ma'am. I'm busted."

"Well, you trot right in alongside o' me. Hurry up, now—ain't got much time to waste. My land, of all the fool men—and at your age! Hurry up."

The two figures departed toward the stirrup-high open flooring that formed a porch the length of the frame building. One was the figure of Dad Griffith. The other was the figure of a very large woman, harsh of features; she was clad in ragged but neat khaki, and beneath her chin were tied the strings of an old black bonnet. Against her wrinkled features glowed two bright-blue eyes with the brilliancy of living jewels, giving the lie to their surrounding tokens of age. She was unknown to Fred Ross.

Filling his pipe, the homesteader sought out the store, and, with inevitable delays, set to work making his purchases. This was an occupation demanding ceremony. Other men were here on the same errand, and there was gossip of crops, land, and war to be swapped. This was the forum of the countryside, the agora of the scattered ranches.

Thus it happened that by the time Ross went to his car with an armload of supplies old Dad Griffith had finished his meal and was lounging on the steps of the stirrup-high porch. He started up at sight of Ross, who paid no attention to him, and followed the rancher out to the car.

"Hey!" he exclaimed, eagerly. "Where's that there partner of mine?"

Ross dumped his purchases into the car and turned. He desired only to be rid of this parasite, to be rid of him for good and all—and to rid Thady Shea of him.

"He's where you left him, old-timer—and where you're not wanted."

"Is—is he all right?"

"Sure. I fed him whiskey until he got well. He's there now with a demijohn. I never seen a man able to swallow more red licker than that partner of yours! But you needn't go showing your nose around there, savvy? He's workin' for me and you're not wanted."

"You go to hell!" spluttered the wrathful ancient. "You goshly-gorful old ranch hand! That's what you are!"

Ross laughed, swung about to his flivver, and cranked up. He turned the car and vanished amid a trail of dust, leaving the ancient to sputter senile threats and curses. He accounted himself well rid of that old vagabond, in which he was quite right.

It was late in the afternoon when Ross got home; the trail to his cañon from the county road was wretchedly rough. As he drove, he began to blame himself for having left Thady Shea all alone, throughout the day from sunrise to sunset, with that wicker demijohn. He began to think that he had stacked the cards too heavily. He began to think that his desire to test Thady Shea had been a mite too strong.

He drove up to the shed, seeing no sign of his guest. The house, too, was deserted. Ross went straight to the corner cupboard and jerked open the door. The clean wicker demijohn was gone. It was not in the house.

"Hell's bells!" quoth Ross, savagely.

He strode outside and scanned the vicinity. Nothing was in sight. The team was gone. He walked up the cañon, seeing that the lower flat was empty of life. At the turn he came in sight of the upper flat, and paused.

The team was there; Thady Shea had been plowing. Thady Shea was there, too, but he was not plowing. He was standing at one corner of the flat beside a pile of brush. He was lifting something in his hand. It was the wicker demijohn. He set it on his arm and laid the mouth to his lips. Ross could see him drink, gulpingly. He drank long, avidly, until Ross swore in blank amazement that a man could drink thus; he drank as the sun-cracked earth drinks water.

Ross strode forward. Thady Shea turned to meet him.

"Hello, Ross! I was just knocking off work for the day. Drink?"

Ross took the demijohn. He looked at Thady Shea with hard, bitter cold eyes. His eyes softened as he remembered his misgivings. After all, was it not his own fault? He lifted the demijohn on his arm and laid the mouth to his lips.

"Hell!" He spluttered in stark surprise. He stared at the demijohn, stared at the smiling Thady Shea. "Hell! I thought—"

Thady Shea laughed. It was a deep, sonorous laugh.

"I couldn't stand it, Ross," he said. "That cursed jug was too much for me. So I emptied out the whiskey and filled it with water, and went to work. I'm sorry about the whiskey—I'll pay you back."

"Damn the whiskey!" roared Fred Ross, delightedly, and wiped his lips. "Come on back to the shack and let's eat!"

For the first time in long days, the two men talked over their meal. They talked of the world outside, talked of ranch gossip, talked of the war and the government and the high price of wool. Ross meant to run some sheep up at the head of the cañon, and discoursed on the project at length. Not until their pipes were going, and the red afterglow was shrouding the fading day, did he mention what he had learned at Datil.

"Heard something over to the hotel," he mentioned, casually. "They were talking about you. It appears that Abel Dorales has called off the sheriff and withdrawn all charges agin' you. He's lookin' for you his own self, I hear. Makin' it a personal matter."

Thady Shea drew a deep breath. Nothing to fear from the law, then! The more personal menace of Abel Dorales he did not consider at all.

"I'll tell you what happened—if you don't mind," he said, diffidently. It was the first time, since that day when he had felled Ross with the cup, that personalities had been touched upon between them.

He told his story. Ross made no comment whatever; in that story he perceived that Thady Shea was a queer, impulsive child, a man whose fear and reason were overruled by his impulses, a man whose primitive soul arose in a lonely grandeur of sincerity, of absolute and wonderful sincerity. Ross felt awed, as a man feels awed when confronted by the mystery of a child's soul.

The name of Mehitabel Crump meant nothing to the rancher; he had perhaps heard of her in past years, but had forgotten her name. When Thady Shea fell silent, Ross knocked the dottle from his pipe and filled it anew.

"You watch out for Dorales," he said. "I know him. He's bad med'cine."

"So everyone says," returned Shea, gravely serious. "I hadn't found it so."

Ross seemed to discern humour in this, and chuckled. "Think ye'll stay here, Shea? Glad to have ye."

"Unless something turns up—yes. I—well, I haven't found that purpose we spoke about once. I'm trying hard. I'm trying to find it, to make it come, to figure out what I must do. Yet I seem all helpless, bewildered—"

"I never heard of any one puttin' a rush label on Providence, not with any success to mention," said Ross, dryly. "You're lookin' so hard for something that you can't find it. You're too damn serious. About sixty, ain't ye? Well, at sixty you're goin' through what ye should ha' gone through at thirty or less. Limber up your joints an' take it easier, pardner. Wait for what turns up, an' remember God ain't dealing from a cold deck."

Here was wisdom, and Thady Shea tried to accept it.

Upon the following afternoon Thady Shea was laboriously plowing the upper flat. Down at the shack, Fred Ross was cleaning house. He was cleaning house in his own simple and thorough fashion. He took everything outside in the sun. Then he set to work with a bucket of suds and a broom, and scrubbed the walls, floor, and ceiling; he was figuring on papering the walls a little later. The result of this cleaning was damp but satisfactory.

Having returned most of his belongings to their proper places, Ross was engaged in fitting together the iron bed. He heard the grinding roar of a car coming up the cañon trail in low gear, and went to the doorway. A dust-white flivver was approaching. As he watched, it came up to the shed and halted. There was but one person in the car.

From the dust-white flivver alighted a tall, large woman clad in old but neat khaki, upon her head a black bonnet. With surprise, Ross recognized her; it was the woman whom he had seen at Datil the previous day. It was the woman who had bought Dad Griffith a meal, and who, presumably, had given the ancient a lift toward the Arizona line.

She approached the doorway and transfixed Ross with keen, glittering blue eyes. Her look was one of unmistakable truculence, of hostility.

"Your name Ross?" she demanded.

"It is, ma'am," he meekly answered. "Will—"

"My name's Mehitabel Crump, with a Mrs. for a handle," she stated. "You got a man by the name o' Shea workin' here?"

"Yes'm," said Ross, staring. So this was the Mrs. Crump of whom Shea had spoken! "Yes'm. Will ye come in? I'll go right up the cañon and fetch him—"

"You shut up," she snapped, harshly. "I aim to do my own fetchin', and I aim to have a word with you here and now, stranger. I hear you been keepin' Thady Shea filled up with booze."

Ross was staggered, not only by the amazing appearance of this woman here, but by her direct attack. She meant business, savage business, and showed it.

Those last words, however, suggested an explanation to Ross. On the previous day he had given the ancient an "earful" about Thady Shea and the whiskey. This woman, who now turned out to be Shea's friend Mrs. Crump, had given the ancient a ride westward. The connection was too obvious to miss.

"You got all that dope from old Griffith, eh?" he said. "I was at Datil yesterday and seen you there. If I ever see that old fool Griffith again, I'll poke a bullet through him!"

"Then you ain't real liable to do it," said Mrs. Crump, grimly. "If that old vagabone told me the truth, I aim to put you where you won't give whiskey to no more men. Now, hombre, speak up real soft and sudden! Did you give Thady Shea whiskey—or not?"

In the blue eyes of Mrs. Crump was a look which Ross had not seen since the days of his boyhood. Even then he had seen it only once or twice, before the "killers" of the old days were put under sod. Knowing what caused that look, Ross laughed—but he laughed to himself.

"Well," he responded, gravely, "in a way it is true, ma'am. I sure did fill Shea with red licker, filled him plumb to the brim. And when I went to Datil yesterday, there was a jug two thirds full o' licker in that cupboard. When I come home las' night, ma'am, there wasn't a single drop o' whiskey left. For a fact."

Try as he might, he could not keep the twinkle from his eye. That twinkle was something Mrs. Crump could not understand; it bade her go slow, be cautious. She knew her type of man animal, and that twinkle gave her covert warning not to make a fool of herself.

"I'm goin' to see him," she declared, after compressing her lips and eying Fred Ross suspiciously. "If you've made a soak out o' him, pilgrim Ross, I'm coming right back here and perforate you without no further warning. That goes as it lays—so ile up your gun."

She turned about and strode away, up the cañon. Once she glanced back, to see Ross standing where she had left him, and upon his face was a wide grin.

CHAPTER XI

THADY SHEA DISCOVERS A PURPOSE

"WHAT IN hell made you run off?" demanded Mrs. Crump in an aggrieved tone.

"Well," hesitated Thady Shea, "I figured I might get you into trouble with Mackintavers and his crowd; Dorales would be after me, you know. And then I wanted to make up for what I'd done. I wanted to go away and prove to myself that I could do something—without any one else helping me. It's a little vague, but—"

"Oh, I savvy," finished Mrs. Crump for him. "My land, Thady! I been hunting you all over creation, but I never aimed to see you lookin' like this—never!" Hands on her hips, she surveyed him with appraising, delighted eyes.

As he stood there awkwardly beside the plow, Thady Shea did look unlike her last view of him. Also, he sounded different. They had talked at length, but in all their talk, in all his tale to date, he had not once broken into the rolling, rounded phrases which formerly he had so loved.

He showed the lack of self-consciousness that was upon him. It was not the bristly beard which had wrought the change, although this disguised him startlingly. Perhaps it was the gruelling work which he had been doing of late, with its effects.

In this man of fifty-eight there showed a strange boyishness. He was no longer gaunt and haggard. True, there was a haunting gentleness, a sadness, in his eyes, but it was the sadness of time past, not of the present. His look, his manner, had taken on a definite personality. No longer was he Thaddeus Roscius, the actor who fitted himself into the characters of other men; Montalembert was dead and here stood Thady Shea, man of his hands; one whose eyes met the world honestly and earnestly, with wide questioning, with a balanced poise and surety in self.

"My land!" pursued Mrs. Crump, meditatively. "When I think of the knock-kneed, blear-eyed critter I found layin' up above the Bajada grade, I can't hardly recognize ye, Thady! Ye look's if ye'd got used to leaning on yourself. Want to come back to Number Sixteen with me?"

Shea frowned in perplexity. His eyes were serious. He had set forth all that had happened to him, all that he had done; Mrs. Crump had given him no blame, but in her eyes had shone pride and praise.

"I—I don't know," he said, slowly. "I'm looking for a purpose in life. I'm trying to find something definite. It's so long since I've had anything definite! These twenty years, and more, there has seemed to be a knot gripped about my soul, somewhere—stifling me. I don't seem to—"

"No need for all that," said Mrs. Crump, impatiently. "You're rich now."

Shea's eyes widened. "You mean—the mine?"

"No, I don't. That mine is a humdinger, or will be once it gets started to paying. I got Lewis an' Gilbert workin' there now, they bein' out o' jail and shut o' that old charge. No, Thady; I mean the ten thousand we screwed out o' that skunk Mackintavers."

Shea looked blank. "Ten thousand? I don't understand."

Mrs. Crump sighed in resignation, and set herself to explain.

"It was a right smart trick to indorse that check Dorales had made ready for ye—'bout the smartest thing I ever knowed ye to do, Thady. I takes that check and lights out and cashes it 'fore old Mackintavers heard what had happened to Dorales. The money's in your name, down to the First National at Silver City; I ain't touched it."

She fumbled in her bosom and produced a folded check book.

"Here's the check book they give me, all proper. Sign your checks the same way ye indorsed that one, savvy? I turned in the note ye left me at the shack, with your signature on it, to the bank."

She broke off. She came to a faltering but decided halt.

For, as she had spoken, a queer look had stolen across the beard-blurred features of Thady Shea, and had settled there. It was such a look as she had never previously seen upon his face. It was a look of incredulous wonder, of grief, of dismay.

The personal equation in that look silenced and startled Mrs. Crump. It conveyed to her that she must have said some terrible thing, something which had shocked Thady Shea beyond words, something which had struck and hurt him like a blow. She rapidly thought back—no, she had not even sworn!

"What the devil ails ye?" she demanded.

"Why—why—that check!" blurted Shea. He drew back from the check book which she was extending to him. His eyes were wide, fixed. "I never meant it—that way! I never dreamed you'd do anything with it. I left it there with the other paper to show you what Dorales had been up to."

Mrs. Crump laughed suddenly.

"Oh, then I gave ye too much credit? Never mind, Thady—"

"You don't understand!" In his voice was a harsh note, a note of pain. "Don't you realize what you've done? That money—why, it's stolen! It'll have to go back to Mackintavers! It isn't ours."

For the first time in many years Mehitabel Crump was shocked into immobile silence. She was absolutely petrified. She could not believe the words she heard.

"You didn't look at it that way, of course," added Shea hastily. Earnestness grew upon him, and deep conviction. "But it's true. If it were ten cents or ten dollars, it might not matter. But—ten thousand dollars! It must go back."

The blue eyes of Mrs. Crump hardened like agates. Her mouth clenched grimly. Her wrinkled features tightened into fighting lines. She was dumbly amazed that the magnitude of the sum did not appeal to Thady Shea's cupidity; but she was vigorously and fiercely determined that the money was to be his. It was not for herself that she wanted it.

When she made answer, it was with a virile insistence that drove home every word like a blow.

"You got no call to insult me, Thady Shea, by callin' me a thief; mind that! Are you crazy or just plain fool? Mackintavers an' Dorales comes along thinking to trim us right and proper, like they done by other poor folks, thinking to rob a lone widder woman, thinking to fool you into robbing me. That there check for ten thousand was the jackpot. Mackintavers signed it as such, knowin' it to be such, stakin' it agin' Number Sixteen to win or lose. You didn't know that the prop'ty was recorded in your name—but he knew!

"He lost, and you can bet he ain't said nothing about losing them table stakes! What call you got to beef about winning that bet? It's plumb legal, cashed at a bank, sanctified by Sandy hisself over the phone. You'd be a fool not to take money after you'd won it in a game like that! If ye want—"

For the second time Mrs. Crump came to a decided and bewildered halt.

She was entirely convinced that to take the money was legitimate; she was convinced that it had been lawfully won, that Thady Shea was actually entitled to it. She had chuckled over the coup a hundred times. She had chuckled a hundred times over the grimly delightful irony of cashing that check, of giving Mackintavers a counter-thrust that he would remember. Yet, although she was presenting her argument with entire conviction, she was conscious that it was like presenting her argument in the face of a stone wall.

Somehow Thady Shea was ignoring her argument. Its point seemed quite lost upon him. He stood before her, flinty, untouched, unheeding. The slight glint of scorn in his eye, real or fancied, flicked Mrs. Crump on the raw; it lashed her into real and unassumed anger.

"All that is quite true," he said. In his manner was a gentleness, a frightful gentleness, a gentleness so entire and calm that it was hideous. One would have said that he was speaking to a little child.

"All that is true, Mrs. Crump. Of course your intentions were whole-souled and generous, and from your viewpoint the action was justified. I didn't mean to call you a thief, heaven knows! I didn't mean any such thing.

"But—the money was to be given in exchange for something. The exchange did not take place. Therefore, to keep the money would be theft. That is the way I look at it. That is all I can see to it—all! The money must go back."

There was a terrible simplicity in the man's face, in the words he used, in the argument he used. It was a simplicity which nothing could change. It was a simplicity above all argument or question. It was a simplicity that stood up like a gray naked rock. Against this implacable front Mrs. Crump was impotent and knew it.

Thady Shea reached out and took the check book from her hand. He opened it. He stripped one check from the book and placed this check in his pocket. Then he took the check book, tore it across, and flung the pieces away. He did it casually, impatiently, carelessly.

Now, to tear a check book across is not an easy thing. To do it carelessly, casually, is a most unusual and significant thing. It jerked at Mrs. Crump's attention. She wondered just how strong Thady Shea was. Yet, the thought that the one check in Shea's pocket was destined for Mackintavers fired the anger within her, and fanned the flame. She could deal gently, pityingly, with a weak man. With a strong man, strong as Thady Shea was strong, she had but one argument.

"I'll write out that check—" began Shea.

"You're a coward!" said Mrs. Crump, savagely. She knew the words were fearfully unjust, but they rose within her and she said them. The thought that Mackintavers would deem her weak and silly enough to return that money maddened her. "You're a coward!"

She leaned forward and struck him in the mouth. She struck a man's blow, a full, hard-fisted, strong blow, a blow that might have felled another man than Thady Shea. Under it he reeled. Then he came upright and stood motionless, looking at her. He did not speak. Slowly he lifted his hand to his mouth, and his eyes shifted to the red smear upon his hand. Then his gaze went again to her face.

Under his look, Mrs. Crump shivered a little. The anger went out of her suddenly and utterly. Before his calm, hurt strength she recoiled. Her brittle, false hardness was broken and shattered. He did not speak, and his silence frightened her. She went to pieces.

"Thady!" The words came from her in a breath, a groan. Her burning blue eyes were gone dull and lifeless, dumb with misery, as she realized what she had just done. "Oh, Thady! I—Heaven forgive me, Thady, I didn't mean to do it. I wanted you to have that money."

"I wonder if you really think I'm a coward?" said Shea, curiously calm. "I am one, of course, but I don't see how a desire for justice can be cowardly."

"I don't!" she burst forth impetuously, passionately. "Thady, I'm sorry—I never meant it; it didn't come from the heart, Thady! I'm an old fool of a woman, that's what I am. An old fool of a woman! Don't look at me that way; I tell ye I can't stand it—it's awful! I'm sorry for it, bitter sorry."

"I'm sorry, too," said Shea, simply. "Listen to me, now. You've given me something real; a purpose. Maybe Ross was right. Maybe I had to wait till it came to me. Now I'm going to find Mackintavers and give him his money, make things right. I may be a coward in physical things, but—"

"Don't talk that way!" she broke in, harshly. "Thady, I'm sorry. Come back to the mine with me; forget this foolishness. I'm a fool of an old woman, that's all. I need ye at the mine, Thady."

He smiled a little. "Do you really mean it, Mrs. Crump? May I come back—after I have seen Mackintavers?"

"Come now! Don't go chasing off like a dratted mule. Come back with me now!"

"No." Shea looked away from her. He motioned toward the horses, their tails switching in the arrogant sunlight. He motioned toward the half-plowed field. "I'll finish this job first. Then, in a few days, I'll go and see Mackintavers. You see? I have to do it. The purpose has come to me; maybe it'll lead into something else. I don't know. After that, I'll come back to Number Sixteen and go to work, if you still want me."

"Yes," she said, humbly. "I'll need ye, Thady. I'm sorry ye won't come now."

She turned from him and walked down the cañon. Around the bend, out of Shea's sight, she leaned against a bowlder. She was a woman, and God has given tears to women. Great sobs shook her for the first time in years. Passionate sobs were they, holding the pent-up emotion of a deep spirit that had broken through its mask of cynic harshness.

Presently Mrs. Crump recalled that, although she was beyond the sight of Thady Shea, she was in full view of the distant shack. Muttering that she was a dratted old fool, she wiped her eyes. She tucked in loosened wisps of hair about the edge of her bonnet. She pulled her bonnet straight and started for the dust-white flivver, beyond the shack.

Mrs. Crump found Fred Ross cheerfully whistling "Silver Threads Among the Gold" and finishing his house-cleaning.

"That there Thady Shea," she stated, harshly, "is the most amazing human critter I've ever run up against!"

Ross grinned amiably. "Meaning, ma'am?"

"Meaning you can figger it out for yourself. Adios!"

"Hold on, ma'am. Ain't you goin' to set a while?"

"I am not. I got work to do. So long, and good luck to ye!"

Ross insisted upon cranking the dust-white flivver, and she departed with no more words.

An hour later Thady Shea brought in the horses, and put them up for the night. He came into the house and helped Ross get supper. He commented on the house-cleaning with admiration. He discussed, from an amateur's standpoint, fencing the upper end of the cañon against the proposed flock of sheep. He seemed to enjoy his supper hugely.

The meal over, both men lounged outside, smoking and watching the crimsoned peaks that overhung them.

"Mrs. Crump," observed Shea at last, "is the most generous, whole-souled woman I ever knew. She's a wonder, Ross!"

"She is," assented the rancher, dryly. "I suppose you're goin' to leave me?"

"Yes," said Shea, gravely. "After that upper flat is plowed."

"Tell you what. Wait till Sunday. I'm goin' to Magdalena then, to see a lady friend. Take ye in the car if you're goin' that way. Then I'll pay you—got to give you something for the work, Shea. So go to Magdalena with me Sunday."

"Mackintavers' ranch lies over there, doesn't it?"

"North. Yes."

"All right. That'll suit me."

CHAPTER XII

THE STONE GODS VANISH

THE LOSS of ten thousand dollars was not a negligible matter, even to Sandy Mackintavers, who was accustomed to gambling on a large scale. Like a good gamester, he swallowed the bitter pill and said nothing. However, the loss left a scar which, contrary to the custom of scars, grew more red and angry with each passing week.

The realization that he had been outwitted and outgamed by the despised Mehitabel Crump was bad enough; the actual monetary loss made itself more gradually felt. However, Mackintavers knew that he would recoup tenfold once his hands gripped Number Sixteen. So, by means of various reports from Eastern sources, he discovered that Coravel Tio, the curio dealer of Santa Fé, was negotiating for the sale of the property, and held an interest in the mine. Over this, Mackintavers laughed long and loud—and perfected his plans for taking over Number Sixteen.

In the meantime, he gave his attention to the seven stone gods and his scientific reputation.

His ranch house was a roomy, comfortable place; one half was inhabited by Old Man Durfee, who ran the ranch, and the other half was inhabited by Sandy and his frequent guests. At the present moment he had three guests besides Abel Dorales. Two were withered, wrinkled old bucks from the Cochiti pueblo, and these were quartered in the bunk house a half mile distant, by the corrals. The third was the eminent archæologist previously mentioned, who had arrived to witness the establishment of Sandy as a scientist.

"To-morrow is the big day, eh?" Sandy Mackintavers spread his square bulk to the blaze in the big library fireplace, and surveyed his scientific guest with complacent expectation. "Dorales is goin' to bring them bucks up here. We'll have the little gods all ready, then we'll see what happens."

He glanced at the wide mantel whereon sat seven worn stone images, grinning widely over the room.

"You've not coached them, of course?" demanded the wary scientist. "If they had an inkling of what you wanted, they'd say anything to please you."

"Huh!" snorted Mackintavers with honest indignation. "I should say not! Surprise is the thing, professor. Aiblins, now, I'll explain to ye the system we've invented to make these Cochiti bucks talk—but first, take a look at this. I'm coming fast, eh? Aiblins, in another year or two I'll be having a world-wide reputation, eh? Just look at this, now."

He handed the scientist a letter. Now, Mackintavers himself could not read that letter; but it had been translated for him, and he was inordinately proud of it.

The scientist glanced at the letter-head above, a large and flaunting letter-head of the *Société Académique,* and below, in very small letters, the remainder of the legend: *d'ethnologie Amerique.* In other words, not particularly good French, denoting the Academic Society of American Ethnology, of Paris.

The eminent scientist repressed the smile that rose to his lips. It was obvious that Sandy, keenly canny in most things, was highly susceptible to this sort of flattery.

"I'm sending for their gold medal," went on the speaker. "Costs about fifteen bucks, but I guess it'll be worth it when the papers write me up, eh? They sent along an engraved parchment to show I'm a member. Some day I'll go to Paris and visit 'em."

The eminent scientist, who knew all the ins and outs of that game, did not spoil poor Sandy's dream by any intrusion of cold and hard facts. Instead, he reflected to himself upon the odd twists and quirks of character, which would bring such a man as Sandy Mackintavers into the toils of a vain ambition, and into the nets of smooth sharpers who knew well how to flatter the American ignoramus into parting with his dollars.

Cordial and warm was Sandy Mackintavers that evening, expanding under the genial thought of what was to happen on the morrow, and making himself a wondrous fine host. He told how Abel Dorales had secured an interpreter, had approached two withered, wrinkled old Cochiti bucks who loved round silver dollars, and had brought them here upon specious pretexts. He told how, on the following morning, those two withered, wrinkled Cochiti bucks were to be left for an hour in this same room, alone with the seven stone gods on the mantel and a whiskey bottle on the table; and he told how a dictagraph, already concealed and in readiness, would be waiting for them.

Being presumably alone, being mellowed by one or two stolen drinks, being in the amazing presence of those seven stone gods, the two withered, wrinkled old Cochiti bucks would most unquestionably talk to each other in their own language. Later, the dictagraph record could be translated.

It never occurred to Sandy that the entire Cochiti pueblo might have been aware that he was in possession of these seven stone gods almost from the very day he obtained them. Sandy had picked up some knowledge about the relics of dead redskins; but he had a good deal to learn about Indians in the flesh.

So the morning came—the morning that was to bring about the satisfaction of ambition. Abel Dorales left the breakfast table in order to bring the two withered, wrinkled old Cochiti bucks. Mackintavers drew the eminent scientist into the library for a last look at the preparations—ah!

"It might be an excellent idea," said the professor, dryly, "to set your stone gods in place, Mr. Mackintavers."

"Aiblins, yes!" And Mackintavers stared blankly at the mantel. "Where the devil have they gone? They were here last night!"

That the seven stone gods had sat, grinning, upon the mantel only the evening previous, was true; but they were not on the mantel now. They were not in the room. They were not in the ranch house at all!

Curious to incoherence, suspecting everyone around him, Sandy Mackintavers sought an explanation. He obtained none. The two wrinkled, withered old bucks had been in the bunk house all night. Every man about the place established a convincing alibi.

Every building upon the place was searched from ground to rafters, without avail. Noon came, and Mackintavers had relapsed into a dour, grim rage. At this juncture, the old Chinaman who served as cook related that, while emptying the slops the previous evening, he had seen a strange horseman down near the creek. He could give no description.

"Stolen!" howled Sandy, beside himself with fury. "Out and after him!"

Now ensued confusion great and dire. Every man on the ranch, except the cook and Abel Dorales and the eminent scientist, shared the general exodus. Dorales openly expressed profound disgust for gods, for Mackintavers, and for the whole accursed business; having assumed responsibility for the safe return of the two wrinkled, withered old Cochiti bucks, he loaded them into the ranch flivver and set out for Socorro and the main line of the railroad. Sandy and Old Man Durfee were gone with the big car.

The professor, left alone, secured a volume of scientific reports and settled himself in comfort on the wide, screened veranda. The noon meal had not been pleasant. The afternoon was hot and dusty. Presently the scientific gentleman slept.

Just when his slumbers had deepened into snoring somnolence, the archæologist was aroused by a sonorous bass voice that boomed like a bell. Startled, he sat up. He first visualized a buckboard close at hand, within a dozen feet of the veranda—a strange thing, for he well knew that natives of the country

would have driven their teams to the corrals. Upon the seat of
the buckboard was a suitcase.

It was a small wicker suitcase, a battered little yellow suitcase
with loose ends of wicker torn and protruding from its faded
surface; it was a suitcase manifestly third or fourth-hand, cheap
in the first place, and now absolutely contemptible. It looked
more like a lunch basket than a suitcase.

Then the professor was aware of a tall man, a large, shaggy-
bearded man, who stood at the screen door of the veranda and
spoke in sonorous accents.

"Sir, it grieves me thus to break your slumber, but I am
searching with such power as lies within my soul for one named
Mackintavers. I charge you, if you be fair Scotia's son and him
whom I do seek, declare yourself!"

"Bless my soul!" exclaimed the scientist. "Do I gather that
you are looking for Mr. Mackintavers?"

"Such indeed are my intent and purpose," declaimed Thady
Shea.

"He's gone. Everyone's gone." The professor inspected this
specimen of humanity with swiftly growing interest. "They'll
be back presently; things are a bit upset. Won't you come in?
Better take your team over to the corrals."

The scientist rose and introduced himself. Thady Shea sol-
emnly gave his abbreviated cognomen and stated that, since he
had hired the team at Magdalena and expected to return almost
at once, the horses could stay where they were. He then entered
the screen veranda, shook hands, and with a sigh sat himself
down.

Mackintavers gone! It upset all his calculations. However,
he soon found himself engaged in sprightly discourse.

Lemonade and cigars made an incongruous accompaniment.
This entire situation, in fact, was the most incongruous the
professor had ever experienced. He could not make out whether
Thady Shea were here as a guest or as an enemy, as a chance

caller, or as a business acquaintance. Thady Shea kept a tight mouth on some things.

"You'd better take those horses into the shade," reiterated the professor at length. "And that suitcase of yours—why, the sun will broil it!"

Thady Shea smiled slightly.

"I perceive dust upon the horizon," he said, gesturing toward the road, "which doth to my mind betoken the speedy return of our host, and the conclusion of my business. As for the suitcase, sir, therein lie food for musing!"

"What's in it then?" The professor chuckled. "A set of Shakespeare?"

"Nay, sir, of its contents I am ignorant."

Thady Shea eyed the approaching dust cloud, which might give birth either to Mackintavers or to Abel Dorales. In his own fashion, he proceeded to tell his companion how he had acquired that suitcase, two hours previously, and while on his way here.

He had encountered a horse, saddled and bridled and still alive, lying in the road with a broken leg. Of the rider, there had been no sign. A little distance farther on Shea had come upon this battered little suitcase lying in the dust. Whether the suitcase appertained to the vanished horseman could not be told. There had been some sort of accident, yet there was no human being in evidence. All this upon the main highway.

"Did you notice the brand on the animal, or anything which might identify it?" queried the professor, who was well versed in the ways of the country.

Thady Shea had learned enough, also, to notice a few such things. The brand was a queer mark, a queer zig-zag which to him meant nothing. The animal's saddle blanket had been an Indian rug, woven for such use. The bridle had also been woven. Upon the suitcase, however, there was no mark of ownership.

"H'm! Sounds like a Navaho brand," commented the professor, sagely.

At this point, Thady Shea rose and abruptly closed the discussion. The approaching automobile had drawn up.

From the car alighted Sandy Mackintavers, who stood for a moment staring at the buckboard; Old Man Durfee went on with the car to the garage, in the rear of the ranch house. Thady Shea did not need the professor's vouchsafed admonition to know who this square-hewn man was, this man with the square jaw and mouth and figure, this man who turned from the buckboard and came dourly up to the veranda.

"Who's here?" Mackintavers stood in the screen doorway.

"You're Mr. Mackintavers?" Theatricalisms fell away from Thady Shea. He fumbled in his pocket. He produced the check which he had previously filled out. He extended it. "This belongs to you, I think. There was some mistake in the matter. Your check was cashed through a misapprehension."

Mackintavers swept Thady Shea with keen, puzzled eyes; then he glanced at the check.

His square mouth contracted slightly at the corners. Otherwise, not a muscle moved in his face. After an instant he folded the check and glanced up at the professor.

"No luck with the thief," he said, curtly. "That is, unless some of the boys bring in news. There was an accident on the Magdalena trail this morning—a fool Navaho buck was hit by the flivver from Doniphan's ranch. Knocked him and his cayuse to glory. I thought for a time he was our man, but telephoned into town from Doniphan's and found otherwise. Took a look at the horse to make sure. Nothing doing."

His eyes went back to Thady Shea. He held open the door and gestured.

"You're Shea, eh? Come on into the office, will you? Excuse me, professor."

Shea followed his enemy host into the house, and into a small room which served Mackintavers as office and study. Sandy dropped into a chair, motioned Shea to another, and set out a box of cigars.

This greeting left Thady Shea entirely at sea. Mackintavers did not seem to be infuriated; he seemed to understand perfectly all about the check. He seemed alert, precise, cold-blooded, as though this were some ordinary business deal.

"So you're Shea!" he repeated. "Aiblins, now—ye look it. Friend o' Mrs. Crump, eh?"

"I am." Thady Shea began to feel sorry that he had come inside.

"How come you're turning back that money? The old lady feelin' her conscience?"

"I told you, sir, that there had been an error. When the mistake was brought to my attention, I posted straightway hither, seeking you; the money was not mine to store away; reparation was incumbent on me."

"What the hell!" muttered Sandy, with a touch of wonder.

Mackintavers knew men. He could read men at a glance, but Thady Shea was slightly beyond his visual acuity. None the less, he came fairly close to the mark in that he adjudged Shea to be of a simple and wonderful honesty, a man of fundamental virtue. Sandy took for granted that Thady Shea was mentally unbalanced; a theory which would explain this amazing refund, and also the wild stories which were current about the man.

"I hear you own that claim Mrs. Crump is workin', Shea."

"No. It belongs to her." Thady Shea rose to his feet. "We need not prolong this—"

"Oh, don't be in a rush!" soothed Mackintavers, cordially. "Now, I'll have your team attended to, and you'd better stay overnight with us, eh? We'll have a talk, and we'll get squared up on the trouble between you and Dorales—"

Thady Shea looked down at him. Under those eyes Mackintavers fell silent.

"Sir, you are an infernal villain," said Thady Shea calmly. "I want none of your hospitality. There is no trouble whatever, save in your own greed and covetous rapacity. You are an arrant rogue, a caitiff vile; there can be naught between us. Sir, fare-well!"

Thady Shea strode from the room and slammed the door after him.

Sandy Mackintavers sat motionless, completely astounded by this outburst. He looked down at the check in his hand, then looked out the window; he could see Thady Shea climbing into the buckboard and driving off.

"Aiblins, yes; the man's mad!" he reflected. A slow chuckle came to his lips. "And to think I never so much as said thank'ee! If the check's good, now—h'm! Better find out about it. A fool, that's what the fellow is. A loose-brained fool."

He sought the telephone and spoke with the Silver City bank. The check was good.

Later in the afternoon came the first word of the actual thief who had made off with the seven stone gods. One of the men brought in a report that he had found signs of a camp on the creek a mile distant. Mackintavers and Old Man Durfee went out to investigate. They were good at reading signs; they discovered that a man had spent the previous night in this spot, and that he had presumably been an Indian. The tracks of his unshod horse showed a cracked off hind hoof. A few tiny shreds of gray wool showed where his saddle blanket had been laid.

Over the supper table that evening Sandy Mackintavers recounted these results to the archæologist. Abel Dorales had not yet returned from Socorro.

"The gods are gone, professor," he stated, disconsolately. "Clean gone! Aye. D'ye see, the thief, that fellow camped by the creek, was the same Indian who got wiped out by Doniphan's flivver this morning! The same, aye. That saddle blanket was gray, and that horse had the off hind foot cracked. Aye. The Navaho dog was the thief. And now the gods are clean gone! There was no sign of 'em about the horse, and the man himself had nothing. But he took 'em, right enough."

The professor glanced up, roused from his abstraction.

"That's queer!" he ejaculated. Excitement rapidly grew upon him. "Look here, Mackintavers! The man who was here this afternoon, the man Shea—did you notice that queer little grip on his buckboard? He told me he had picked up that grip near the crippled horse, and he did not know what was in it!"

Just then Abel Dorales returned, to find that Thady Shea had come and gone.

Thirty minutes later Mackintavers and Dorales were on their way to Magdalena in the big car; Mackintavers was after the seven stone gods, and Dorales was after Thady Shea.

CHAPTER XIII

THADY SHEA STARTS HOME

IN THE early evening Thady Shea reached Magdalena. He turned in his team and buckboard to the livery stable, paid for its use from the money given him by Fred Ross, and with the little suitcase in his hand left the stable office. The first person he encountered was Fred Ross.

"Hello!" said Ross, grinning. "Thought maybe you'd show up this evenin', so I hung around. How's tricks?"

"Fine," answered Shea, delightedly. "I'm hungry."

"So'm I. Let's eat. I got a friend waitin' to meet ye—he's leavin' to-night."

Shea gladly followed to the Hotel Aragon. He was to-night blissfully happy. For the first time in years he felt like a boy. It was as though the reparation made to Mackintavers, and the brief but emphatic expression of his own mind to Mackintavers, had wiped away all past things. Atonement was over and done with. He was free to go where he would.

From one of the rocking-chairs in the long, narrow lobby of the hotel arose a man of girth and twinkling of eye, who came to meet them. Him Ross briefly introduced as Bill Murray, and urged haste in reaching the dining room. Thady Shea left the battered little yellow suitcase on the hat rack beside the dining-room doors, which were just about to close, and the three men hastily entered the nearly empty room.

Fred Ross had known nothing definite about Thady Shea's business with Mackintavers, but possibly he had conjectured a good deal. He was plainly much relieved to see his friend safely back.

"Bill's running a newspaper over to St. Johns," he confided, when the meal was under way. "He'd heard about you, Shea, and was kind o' set on meeting you. Wants to get the straight o' that yarn about you and Dorales. He got laid up here with a busted steering gear, and aimed to go home to-day, but waited over. Now he's goin' back to-night, so he says. It sure beats all how a fellow gets in a hell of a hurry just when other folks want him to loaf around a spell!"

Murray tipped Thady Shea a jovial wink.

"Fred ain't lonesome, much," he said, wheezily. "Got a girl here. Fred reckons that the more he talks about stayin', the more I'll be set on goin'—which is the same true. Human nature is ornery as the devil, ain't it now? Well, I s'pose you ain't picked up any news to-day, Shea?"

"I have, sir," intoned Thady, "an item of importance. A striped Indian, of name unknown, was overcome by dire fatality this morn. Upon the road Death ambushed him, and maimed his faithful steed, and laid him low. An automobile—mark the irony!—became the instrument of darkling fate, and brought to this poor aborigine the end of all things, and the close of life."

Bill Murray stared open-mouthed, as did most people who heard Thady's sonorously rolling accents for the first time. Then he emitted a wheezy chuckle.

"Oh! You mean the Injun buck that got straddled by Doniphan's flivver! Heard all about him to-day. He's layin' over to the funeral parlours now. Some of his tribe's in town, and they made Doniphan give him a real burial. Joke on Doniphan, ain't it?"

"And," pursued Thady, "at Mackintavers' ranch this afternoon I gathered there had been a robbery. What worldly pelf was taken, I know not, but dread confusion reigned upon the place."

"Gosh!" Bill Murray started up from his chair. "Say—that's red-hot news, Shea! Don't tell any one else around here. I'll run out and phone the ranch. Got to run off my paper to-morrow night; I'll pull some o' that plate off the front page and run this in a box. Whee! Back in a minute!"

Bill Murray departed like a genial cyclone.

Now Thady Shea told about that battered little suitcase. He was not sure what should be done with the thing, and asked the advice of Fred Ross. He had not opened the suitcase; ever since finding it, he had been on the go. Besides, the suitcase was locked, and Thady hesitated to smash it open.

"Likely it was bounced off some ranch car or buckboard," deduced Ross. "Belong to that dead Injun? No chance. None whatever! You never seen an Injun with one o' them things, and anyhow, no Injun riding hossback would tote a suitcase along. No, none whatever! And that grip wasn't made to tie on a saddle, neither. Reckon you'd better look inside, and if there ain't any indication of the owner, then read the papers for an ad. Well, what ye going to do? Will ye come back to the ranch with me?"

Thady Shea did not know what he wanted to do. He wondered if he had fulfilled his extremely vague ideas of wandering and making good in the world. In a sense, he had done so. He realized it now, just as he realized that it is very difficult to view one's own immediate self and environment with any degree of cool detachment.

As to Mackintavers, as to any peril which he himself might bring upon Mrs. Crump, Thady Shea had long since abandoned that nebulous idea. He had met Mackintavers, and feared him no longer. Of Dorales he did not think particularly.

He had no great desire to return to the Ross ranch. Try as he would, he could see no purpose ahead of him save in the one place—Number Sixteen. All that held him back was that strange feeling in his soul, a feeling that had been there twenty years and more; a feeling as though something were knotted somewhere about his soul, stifling him. What use to return to Mrs. Crump? Still, there was the only purpose he could see.

He had conquered the old enemy; of this he felt certain. Temptations would come, of course. Temptations were bound to come; they came at odd intervals; they came here in this hotel dining room, where he could catch some vagrant odour of whiskey from an indefinable source. Yet they would not overcome him anew, he was confident.

"I think," he said, slowly, staring at the tablecloth, "I think I'd better head for Mrs. Crump's mine, Ross."

There was that in his voice which admitted of no argument. Ross shoved back his chair.

"Well, wait a minute, will you? I want to speak to Bill Murray. Order me some o' that pie and another cup o' coffee, Shea."

Fred Ross opened the dining-room doors, which had been closed, and departed to the lobby of the hotel. He found genial Bill Murray just turning from the telephone, and wearing a look of puzzled excitement.

"Get the ranch?" asked Ross. The other nodded and glanced around cautiously.

"Yes. Talked to Old Man Durfee—he's manager for Sandy. He said that Sandy and Abel Dorales had just left for Magdalena; he admitted there had been a robbery but would say nothing except that it didn't amount to much. Injun relics, he said."

"Huh!" Fred Ross gazed at his friend, narrow-eyed. "I bet if it was Injun relics, it was some partic'lar kind, then. That sounds damn' fishy, Bill."

"Sure does, but she'll make a grand little story, played up. This here Shea just came from there, didn't he? And everybody knows about him and Dorales and the bad blood."

The two men looked at each other, surmise in their eyes. Ross thoughtfully rubbed his chin, remembering about that battered little suitcase on the hat rack. He did not entirely believe the tale told by Thady Shea, the tale about finding it in the road. That was too improbable, unless the dead Indian had been carrying the suitcase—which seemed, likewise, very improbable.

"I shouldn't wonder, now," said Ross, musingly. "Shea, he's the calm, hell-nervy sort, he sure is. Likely Dorales or old Sandy tried to run a blazer on him, and he played merry hell with them. Likely they had something he thought belonged to someone else, and he just up and took it. H'm! But the robbery had happened before he got there, he *said*. Well, if he don't want to tell all he knows, that's his business. Eh?"

"I coincide," assented Murray, curtly. Fred Ross briefly told him about the suitcase, in so far as he knew about it.

"Now," pursued Ross, "you and I ain't blamin' him or any other man for gettin' old Mackintavers up on his ear. But Shea, in spite o' the stories goin' around about him, ain't no fighter, Bill. He's a downright honest man, and he's terrible when he gets roused, but I don't guess he could fight for little apples. *And,* he don't know Sandy and Dorales are comin' to town."

"I see," said Murray, thoughtfully. "But he ain't the kind to run away, Fred."

"C'rect. But why should he know anything about Sandy coming? We'd ought to see that he avoids 'em, so to speak. You're goin' west to-night. You got room, ain't you?"

"Oh!" Murray chuckled, admiringly. "So that's the game! Sure, I got room. Where is he goin', though?"

"Near as I got the location o' the mine he's aiming for, it's in the hills above them lava beds, down beyond Zacaton City and No Agua. You're goin' west by the highway, which is north o' there—a long sight north. But if you were to run a few mile out of your way, you could hit down the Old Fort Tularosa trail, which is an auto road now; you could drop Shea by the Beaver Cañon trail, down within thirty mile o' home, more or less. I'll send Sandy and Dorales on to St. Johns after you, savvy?"

For a moment the two men conferred eagerly.

Unobserved by them, meantime, a man had entered the hotel and was standing at the cigar case, at one side of the desk. He was buying cigars. He was roughly dressed, but spoke perfect English. When he turned to the cigar lighter, disclosing his face to view, one could see that he was very swarthy, very dark of colour—an Indian, perhaps.

This man straightened up, puffing at his cigar. His eyes flitted to the little battered suitcase, which reposed on the hat rack, and dwelt there; thus dwelling, his eyes narrowed slightly. He turned and left the hotel.

"Who? Him?" said the hotel proprietor in response to a question from a man near by. "Why, he's Thomas Twofork; yep, an Injun, from Cochiti pueblo, I hear. Been in town two-three days now. Got money, they say, heaps of it."

Ignorant of what had transpired in the lobby, Thady Shea was glad when his companions rejoined him and sat down to their interrupted repast. Fred Ross broached the subject of departure; he broached it with elaborate carelessness.

"Bill is headin' for home right away," he said, "and he goes within thirty mile, more or less, of where your mine's located, Shea. If you figger on walking, that would be a good lift. If you go back with me to-morrow, you won't get near so nigh home."

"Oh!" Thady Shea saw no guile; he looked gratefully surprised, and felt it. He had anticipated a long trip via Zacaton City. That route would be attended with dangers from Dorales or the latter's men, besides having the expense of a car to take him to Number Sixteen.

"Oh! I'd be glad indeed—but do you have to leave to-night?"

"You bet," said Murray, emphatically. "The minute I get this here pie down. I got the ol' car all ready to hike, and I'm goin' to hike some. I aim to get home about sun-up, sleep two-three hours, then get to work on the paper. She's got to be run off to-morrow night, see? And I'd sure be glad o' your company, Shea. It's a lonesome trip at night from here over through Datil Cañon and all."

Surely, thought Shea, here was fate aiding him! Barely had he resolved to seek Mrs. Crump and the mine, than this opportunity offered. A walk of a few miles did not worry him in the least.

"Thank you, Murray," he rejoined. "I'll go, with pleasure."

Ten minutes later, the three men left the hotel, walked up to the corner, and turned in to the garage behind the trading store. Bill Murray paid his debts to the proprietor and sought his own car.

"Well, Ross, I'll say good-bye for a while, at least." Shea turned and shook hands with his friend. "I'll see you again, that's sure. Oh—by the way, hadn't we better open that suitcase? I forgot about it. Let's get it broken open here, and—"

Ross interposed a hasty negation. He wanted only to get Shea safely out of town before Mackintavers and Dorales should arrive.

"No, don't get Murray nervous, hangin' around here, Shea. He's dead anxious to be off, and we better not give him any delay. I'm sure curious about what's in that case, just the same. S'pose you drop me a line when you find out, and give my regards to Mis' Crump! Maybe I'll drift over your way some time; if not, you know where to find me."

"You bet," assented Thady Shea, warmly.

Murray motioned Thady Shea into the front seat, and took the battered little suitcase to shove it into the rear of the car. An ejaculation almost escaped his lips as he felt its weight. It was heavy, tremendously heavy!

"Ore, likely," he muttered. "I bet he don't walk thirty mile with *that!*"

Thady Shea and Fred Ross parted with a last handshake. Each of them had probed deep into the other man; each of them had found the other strangely dissimilar, yet strangely attuned in spirit to himself; each of them had found the other to be a man. Their handshake was firm and quick and strong.

Ross cranked the car. Bill Murray backed her from the garage, roared a last farewell, and headed out into the west and the night.

Fred Ross went back to the hotel after calling upon certain friends of his; for Ross had a fairly good idea of what was coming next. His theories were not altogether correct, but they attained pretty correct results.

So, after a short time, Fred Ross returned to the hotel and sat down in the lobby, just under the big map of New Mexico that hung upon the south wall. Immediately around him the comfortable oak rocking-chairs were vacant; but to right and left, three chairs away, sat red-faced men who read newspapers—two on either hand. These four men displayed an ostentatious lack of interest in each other and in Fred Ross. Over that section of the lobby hung an ill-defined air of crisis, of expectation, of foreboding.

Over opposite, in a corner of the big front window, sat a man, a stranger to Fred Ross. This man had come into town on the late afternoon train. He was palpably a city man, palpably not of this part of the country; he had registered at the desk as James Z. Premble of New York. Speculating idly as he waited, Fred Ross set him down as a high-class drummer.

Thus waited the six men, as though they were awaiting some event about to happen: Ross, seated under the big wall map; the four red-faced men who read newspapers with marked absorption; and, in the corner of the window, James Z. Premble of New York.

Suddenly and abruptly it happened. It happened just as Fred
Ross had anticipated. The hotel door opened and into the lobby
walked Sandy Mackintavers with Abel Dorales at his elbow.
They had been to the livery stable, they had been to one place
and another, and they had soon learned that Thady Shea, easily
noted and remembered by all who saw him, had been in the
company of Ross and Murray. Both Ross and Murray were
known to Mackintavers and his field marshal.

Upon entering, Abel Dorales passed straight on to the cigar
stand, where he stood idly gossiping with the proprietor. Mackintavers, with a wave of his hand and a grunt, halted in front
of Fred Ross, and dropped into a chair beside the latter.

"Hello, Ross. Just the man I was looking for. Know a man
name o' Shea, Thady Shea?"

"Evening," returned Ross, easily. "Sure I know him. Seen him
a while ago."

"Know where he is now?" asked Mackintavers without too
great show of interest.

"Uh-huh. He went off with Bill Murray to St. Johns a couple
of hours ago. Murray was in some hurry, believe me! He'd been
laid up here with a busted car, and had to get out his paper
to-morrow sure pop, so he aimed to travel some to-night. You
interested in Shea?"

"Some." Mackintavers bit into a cigar. Over the cigar, his
eyes fell upon James Z. Premble of New York, who was also
looking at him. After an instant Premble rose and left the hotel.

Ross had not hesitated to impart the information about
Thady Shea, for the excellent reason that if Mackintavers fol-
lowed Shea to St. Johns, he would miss Thady Shea entirely.
Therein Fred Ross made a mistake. It did not occur to him that
Dorales, in a high-powered car, might follow the tracks of
Murray's flivver where it struck from the highroad upon the
Old Fort Tularosa trail.

" 'Bliged to ye, Ross." With this curt speech, Mackintavers
heaved himself out of his chair and went to the door. He passed
out into the night.

Abel Dorales left the cigar stand, and also started for the door. But he stopped before Fred Ross, exchanged a word of greeting, and his white teeth showed in a smile. It was not a pleasant smile.

"I hear you're going to run sheep on your ranch, Ross," he said clearly. "Bad manners for an old cowman, isn't it?"

The four red-faced men laid aside their newspapers. They seemed to take sudden interest in Abel Dorales. Fred Ross looked up, unsmiling, his eyes hard and cold.

"Handsome is as handsome does, Abel. Reckon I'd sooner run sheep than get chloroformed and hogtied tryin' to jump a claim."

A fleeting contraction passed across the face of Abel Dorales. His eyes narrowed to thin slits. His nostrils quivered like the nose of a dog sniffing game. He became white-lipped, cruel, venomous.

The four red-faced men stirred. One of them rose, yawning, and stretched himself as does a weary man who thinks well of bed for the night. Abel Dorales took sudden warning. He looked to the right and to the left; then, without a word more, he turned on his heel and walked away, following Mackintavers out into the night.

"Trust a Mex to smell trouble!" said one of the men to the left of Fred Ross. "He reckoned we was planted to do him up."

"Well, wasn't we?" queried someone. All laughed in unison. Ross smiled grimly and left his chair.

"Much obliged to ye, boys. I didn't know they would come alone, or I wouldn't ha' bothered ye."

Outside the hotel, meantime, Mackintavers had joined James Z. Premble, who appeared to have been awaiting him. A moment later Abel Dorales, mouthing low and vitriolic curses, joined them. In silence the three men turned to the left and walked down to the railroad track. There, beyond the warehouse, they stood with open and empty space around them, and none to overhear.

"Didn't look for ye quite so soon, Premble," said Mackintav-ers, chuckling a little as he used the name.

"Got a good chance at my man," returned the other. "Came in this afternoon, Sandy, but couldn't catch you at the ranch. Ready for me to work?"

"Aiblins, yes; reckon we'd better get busy, you and I." He turned to Dorales. "Abel, our man has gone to St. Johns with Murray. You have plenty o' friends in that Mormon town, so take the big car and mosey along. Do whatever you want with Shea, but bring me back that bunch o' stone gods if ye value your life! I'll be at Mrs. Crump's location."

"All right," snapped Dorales. "Is he much ahead of me?"

"Two hours, in a flivver. You can't fail to land him this time. Good luck, boy!"

Dorales snarled farewell, and swung off in the darkness. Mackintavers turned to his friend, James Z. Premble.

"I'm gettin' old," he complained. "Been out chasin' a thief all day and I'm no good for an all-night ride now. I'll take a room at the hotel. Drop in after a spell and we'll arrange the details. You got the stuff?"

"Every blessed paper and letter. Everything O.K.," asserted Premble.

The two men melted into the night.

Five minutes later Dorales was filling his gasoline tank at the garage. He made brief inquiries about Murray's flivver and the brand of tires thereon. Off to one side, a swarthy man was hastily working upon the fan belt of a big car, which had twice broken as his engine started; this swarthy man took keen and unobserved interest in the questions of Dorales. The name of this swarthy man was Thomas Twofork, and he was an Indian of the Cochiti pueblo. Twenty minutes after Dorales had de-parted Thomas Twofork had finished his repairs and headed his car out upon the westward road to St. Johns.

An hour afterward, well into the night, an automobile came into Magdalena from the opposite direction. It came in by the eastern road, the road that comes up from Socorro through Blue Cañon, the road that comes south to Socorro from Albuquerque and Santa Fé. This automobile did not turn into a garage; instead, it passed on through the business section of the town and did not slacken speed until it reached the Mexican or western quarter.

There it came to a halt and its horn squawked four times. Its searchlight revealed a small adobe house with blue-painted doors. One of these doors opened to show a man clad in dishevelled night attire. The automobile drove on into the yard; its lights flickered out.

"Is that you, Juan Baca?" queried a soft, gentle voice. "Ah, yes; it is I, Coravel Tio. Will you give me lodging for the night?"

"Señor, my house and all it contains belong to you!"

Coravel Tio passed into the little adobe house.

CHAPTER XIV

DORALES KILLS

IN THE chill darkness that precedes the early dawn Thady Shea alighted from Bill Murray's car. Before him, a few miles distant, were Old Fort Tularosa and Aragon; many miles behind was the highway. Down to the southeast—somewhere—was his destination.

"Mind, now," cautioned Murray, "you take this here trail and it'll lead up through them hills into Beaver Cañon. Follow Beaver Crick all the rest o' the way. Near as I can judge, your place is somewhere down beyond Eagle Peak. If you get clear lost, send up a smoke and a ranger will be dead sure to trail you down. G'bye and good luck!"

"Good-bye, and many thanks for the lift!" responded Shea, his sonorous voice pierced with the chill of the early morning. Murray went buzzing away on the back trail.

Carrying his battered little suitcase, Thady Shea started off, gradually accustoming his eyes to picking out the rough trail. It mattered nothing to him that he might be days upon this road; it mattered nothing that he was about to negotiate the continental divide afoot. Time and space did not concern him, nor bodily discomfort. His was the supremely ignorant confidence of a child as he headed into the mountains to find a mine whose entire location, going at it from this direction, was a matter of guesswork.

To be more accurate and practical, Thady Shea, having slept lightly while riding, was weary. He was also cold and confused. Now that he had reached a decision and was really on his way to Number Sixteen, he felt unaccountably homesick. Not that Number Sixteen meant home, but Mrs. Crump would be there. As usual, Thady Shea was a bit vague in analyzing his feelings; but he had a solid and definite purpose in view, at least. He was going to rejoin Mrs. Crump. He was going to learn mining work.

He went on, trudging bravely under his burden, until the cold had pierced and chilled and numbed him. At last he could endure the cold no longer. Ignorant of forest rangers or forest law, he had quite missed the point of Miller's parting joke about sending up a smoke. He contrived to build himself a fire; a fine roaring fire, a ruddy, leaping fire that warmed him. It was a fire that blazed forth patent defiance of all law. Its darting glow was caught by a forest ranger in a lookout on Indian Peaks fifteen miles away.

With the first gleam of the rising sun Thady Shea abandoned his blazing fire and took up his journey again, following the winding trail without trouble. A little later he halted and made a cold breakfast from some of the food that filled his pockets. Then he decided to open the suitcase and see if it were worth carrying farther, or if it held tokens of ownership. By this time, he was sorry that he had dragged the thing along.

He smashed open the suitcase. Within it he found wads of crumpled newspapers, and among the newspapers seven stones.

At first he thought they were nothing but stones. Gradually he realized that they were carven images of some sort. Except for these, there was nothing in the suitcase. There was nothing to denote its ownership—not a mark, not a line, not a card nor a word.

Thady Shea set out the seven stone gods on the ground, and regarded them. The more he looked at them, the more he saw in them. Each one was somewhat different in shape, but all were of a size. They were smooth and rounded, as if from much handling, or as if worn sleek by many centuries. They were crude, uncouth little figures, those gods; they were fashioned rudely in the semblance of man, with every angle and sharp line worn down, obliterated, rounded.

"They look as if some kid had been making mud dolls, and the mud had hardened," observed Shea in some wonder. The description was accurate and perfect.

Thady Shea knew nothing about Indians or their gods. He had not the slightest idea what these things really were; but he was a member of The Profession, an actor of the old school. All his life he had been surrounded by the superstitions of the old school. As everyone knows, there are no stronger, firmer, and more absolute superstitions than those of The Profession.

As Thady Shea gazed upon those seven stone gods which sat in the dust and grinned stonily back at him, various things suggested themselves to his fertile brain. Seven of them—and seven was beyond question a lucky number! Then, fate had undoubtedly placed them in his hand and had removed any clew to their former owners. Luck had come to him, and if he threw the luck away because of a little bother involved in carrying it—well, that would be an ill thing to do!

Out of his subconscious self evolved a curious idea, a remembrance. What did these things represent? He dimly remembered something about the seven heavenly virtues and the seven deadly sins. The vague thought stirred him. These images were ugly enough to represent the seven sins—or the seven virtues.

He must keep them at all costs; in the manner of their coming was something fated, something that appealed to all the latent superstition within him. He dared not refuse these talismen!

So he replaced them in the suitcase and took up his road anew.

It was a rough road that called to him. It was a long and lonely road, a road that took him out of human ken and into the heart of the high hills.

He swung along at a good four-mile clip, his long legs fast covering the ground. He had never before this day been actually among the mountains, and he liked their friendly, forested faces. The rough trail denoted very little usage, yet this absence of all humanity did not oppress Thady Shea. He felt gloriously independent, free!

About noon he was following Beaver Creek through a rough and rugged cañon. Here he lunched, with a silver-black pool of water foaming and bubbling fifty feet below him; a pool that foamed green and silver with sunlight and bubbled with black shadows. Over on the opposite wall of the cañon was a broken line of masonry, half hiding a niche in the rock where once had lived and died the cliff dwellers. It was a spot to remember. It was a place that stirred the deep things in a man's soul, that caused him to think upon the mysteries, the flashing glimpses of occult things. About that place there lingered a sense of the futility of man, a sense of the gorgeously foaming and bubbling eternity of the Creator. Thady Shea was glad that he had seen that place.

Afterward, he halted for a smoke, this time beside the stream itself, farther along the cañon. Thady Shea had never been a boy—until to-day. At ten years he had been an accomplished actor, a child marvel, drunken and drugged with the unhealthy atmosphere of the stage. But now—now! The altitude was high, and he was drunk as with fine wine. He waded in the stony creek, he even thought of fishing with a bent pin on a string; but he had neither pin nor string. He enjoyed a truant hour.

Then he went on his way anew, vowing inwardly that some day he would return to this little bubbling creek and the winding cañon amid the mountains.

Despite the altitude, weariness had left him, and he carried the seven stone gods without feeling their weight. Deeper and lonelier grew his trail, the mountains folding him in upon every side. He began to feel the infinity of distance. He was a mere tiny atom here among these great solitudes. His insignificance was borne home upon him, mellowing all his spirit.

In this chastened mood he came, suddenly and without warning, upon the tragic shack of the sheep-herder.

It was a shack of logs and hewn timbers, a rough little shack, a tragic little shack. Upon one wall was fastened a faded paper, a permit issued by the forest ranger to cut these same timbers. In the sun by the doorway sat a little brown, half-naked baby, perhaps a year of age, whimpering and chewing upon a strip of raw white bacon. There was no one else visible. Over the place, tainting the clear high air, hung a fearful odour of mortality; an odour of tragic suggestion, an odour of blood and liquor.

Seeing no one about except the baby, who stopped whimpering at sight of him, Thady Shea advanced to the doorway. He glanced inside. As he did so, cold and awful horror stiffened upon him. Even to his tyro's eye the story was plain to read.

Upon the bare earthen floor, just inside the door, sat the sheep-herder. The effluvia of his garments told eloquently his profession. Between his outstretched feet lay a cheap revolver. His swarthy, brutal face, the face of a Mexican, the face of a barbarian drawn from mingled Indian and bastard Spanish blood, was sunken upon his chest. He was breathing stertorously, horribly. He was drunk, stupefied with liquor. Upon the floor beneath his hand had fallen an empty bottle which stank of the vilest mescal.

Only a few feet distant, sprawled under one wall of the room, was the body of a woman, a brown native woman. She had been upon her knees beneath a little crucifix. She had fallen partly forward, partly sideways; a cotton garment had been torn from her left shoulder and breast, as though in some last agony. Beneath the left breast, black with flies, a pool of black blood was coagulating. She had not been dead a long time; an hour or two, no more.

Thady Shea took a step backward. He put one hand to his eyes, as if to shut from his vision that sordid and horrible scene. For a moment he stood thus, his brain in riotous turmoil; then he started violently as a hand touched his arm.

"Hello, stranger! I been looking for you!"

Shea stared at the man who had just dismounted from a pony; a white man, grave and steady of eye. Something in the horror-smitten face of Shea drew an exclamation from this other man.

"Here—what's the matter?"

"In there. Look!" Thady Shea motioned to the doorway.

The other man, the forest ranger who had come from the lookout station on Indian Peaks, quickly strode forward. His figure filled the doorway for a long moment. He stood there silently, gazing in upon that tragic shack, reading every detail with skilled eyes. At last he turned and rejoined Thady Shea, who was staring down at the baby.

"You built a fire early this morning on the old trail up from the Tularosa Road?" The ranger gave his name and office. "H'm-m. Know anything about the fire laws?"

"Fire laws? No," Shea was disturbed and wondering. "Why? Shouldn't I have built any fire?"

"Not that kind—not a big hell-roarer. No harm done, I reckon; I stamped out your fire. But see to it that you don't do it again. Here's a copy of the laws."

He extended a card. Shea pocketed it with a helpless gesture, and looked again at the doorway of the shack. The ranger caught his look, and nodded.

"I guess you'd just found 'em, eh? It's a hell of a note. This fellow Garcia, with his wife and kid, came up from Mexico; refugees. He's been herding some sheep; some that the Y Ranch got a permit to run in a big box cañon last winter—and he's not a bad sort when he's sober. But now—well, there's no doubt about him now. He'll be a good greaser in two-three weeks, when the drop's sprung. Suppose I got to take him in; hell of a note! You ain't been inside?"

Thady Shea shuddered. "No," he answered. He looked down at the baby. The baby looked up at him, removed the strip of white bacon from her mouth, and smiled.

"It's a girl!" said Thady Shea in surprise and awe.

The ranger gave him a curious look, then took out his note-book and pencil.

"Name and where from, if you please," he said. "We'll likely have to come and take down your testimony later on."

Thady Shea gave his name, and gave as well as he was able the location of Mrs. Crump's mine. The ranger once more eyed him, but this time with a new air.

"Hell! I've heard o' you, Shea. Partners with Mrs. Crump, eh? That's a pretty good recommend. Where you goin' from here?"

"To the mine. I believe that by following this creek I'll get into the right territory sooner or later. I know how to reach the mine from Zacaton City, but from this direction I'm not so sure."

Thady Shea was badly off. He was thoroughly shaken by the fearful scene within the tragic shack. It had unnerved him, and he wanted a drink with avid and terrible longing. The ranger observed it.

"I ain't offering you any drinks, Shea," he said, drily. "Heard a few things about what happens to folks that offer you drinks. Still, I always do carry a drop for emergencies, and I have a notion that you need a sip mighty bad."

Thady Shea forced a grim smile. "Thanks. But—the need will have to be greater than it is now, my friend. You think I can reach the mine to-night?"

"No. Some time to-morrow, most likely. Now listen close and I'll give you directions where to leave this cañon, or else you'll come out clear down on the Gila!"

Having gleaned a fairly precise knowledge of the location of Number Sixteen, the ranger proceeded to give Thady Shea an accurate mental map of the trails, backed up by a rough drawing. Then he entered the shack, carried out the murderer, and bound the man on his pony like a sack of flour.

"What the devil will become o' the kid?" he queried. "Come on, Shea, let's get the poor woman buried. That baby, now—d'you suppose you could wait here until I send back for her? I can't handle the greaser and the baby, too."

Thady Shea did not respond at once. He seemed oblivious of the question; but as a matter of fact, he was deep in thought.

The two men together dug a grave and decently interred the poor murdered woman. Over the mound Thady Shea intoned a fragmentary burial service. What he lacked in words he made up in rolling phrases culled from other sources than the prayer book, and in a deeply sincere manner which sat upon him with stately dignity.

They returned to the front of the shack, where the ranger rolled a cigarette with studied care, and returned to his perplexity.

"What about this here kid, now? These folks haven't any kin this side the border, and these greasers don't give a whoop for babies anyhow; too common. This Garcia is the one that deserves my close and personal attention until he gets shoved into the kind o' hell he's bound for—which won't be very long. Of course, the kid can go to some orphanage or the State will take care of her. She's a smilin' little cuss!"

Thady Shea fingered his shaggy, gray-black beard.

"If there's a razor around the place, I think I'll shave," he uttered, thoughtfully. His words drew a look of frowning surprise from the ranger, so utterly at variance with the subject did they seem. "Yes, I think I'll shave."

"Why, friend, I've been thinking about that infant," pursued Shea. "You know Mrs. Crump, I gather? I think she would care for the little one. I'll take care of the child on the journey there; I imagine we can get along. I—er—I don't mind saying that— er—there is a whimsey born of infancy's fond smiles which warms the kindlier soul within a man."

He broke off, quite at a loss for further words. But the ranger understood, and smiled to himself.

"That suits me, Shea. You'll be at the mine, eh? May call on you later in regard to the evidence here. Yes, that's a good plan. Let's see if we can chase up a razor, now."

The ranger disappeared inside the tragic shack.

Upward of two hours later a new Thady Shea was continuing his journey; the tragic shack was far lost to view in the wilderness behind him.

His upper lip, his long under jaw, were shaven and in white contrast with the bronzed skin of cheeks and brow. His wide, mobile mouth and chin differed from those of the wastrel Thaddeus Roscius who had lain in the road above the Bajada hill. They were firmer, more virile of set, stronger of muscle.

In one hand he carried the battered little yellow suitcase. Upon the other arm was perched the half-naked brown baby, for whose benefit Shea also carried a blanket tied to his shoulders. This was not the ideal trim for a walking tour across the Continental Divide, but Thady Shea had no complaints to make.

Never before had Thady Shea communed alone with a baby, particularly with a baby quite dependent upon him. This baby could not talk but she could coo, and she did coo. She could laugh, and she did laugh. She seemed to find a kinship within the deep, sadly earnest eyes of Thady Shea. She made it evident that she liked his eyes, and whenever they were turned upon her, she giggled with self-conscious and adorable delight.

The day wore on. When darkness descended, Thady Shea camped at the brink of the cañon, at the edge of a deep and stony gully which ran down into the cañon below. He built a fire, this time in accord with the laws of the land, and produced his scant store of food. Fortunately, the baby was used to living by rough ways and pastures sere.

In this one day Thady Shea lived long years. He realized it himself. He realized the change within him; he perceived it at once, without any vagueness or obscurity. He was filled with wonder and awe. He felt clearly that the manifest friendship and love of this brown baby had loosened something far inside of him. Within a few hours she had loosened something which had been hard and clenched and bitter inside of him these twenty years—something like a knot gripped about a part of his soul, stifling it. But now, at last, the knot was loosened, was gone.

Once again he fell asleep under the stars with glinting tears bedewing his brown cheeks; they were tears of joy and thankfulness. He knew that he was no longer to drift upon the earth. From depending upon the applause of others for happiness, others were now depending upon him. He had someone for whom to live. Vanity was gone from him, and the worth of life was come in unto him. He now had a purpose, a real purpose, to drive him.

That this purpose was very definite and earnest, he had realized with the unloosing of that knot about his soul. He knew whither he was going, and why—why he wanted to find Mrs. Crump. He fell asleep with tears upon his cheeks and in his heart a dumbly vibrant song.

Some time during the night he was awakened; the baby was whimpering, was cold. The fire was dying down. He had been awakened by a queer noise, a noise like the clank of a shod hoof against a stone. He rose and kicked the ember ends into the fire. He removed his coat and laid it over the baby, then he stood looking down at the bundle. The fire flickered up until its glowing flare lighted his tall figure redly and distinctly.

From somewhere in the darkness came a slight sound. Thady Shea lifted up his head and peered about, the vague thought of wild animals disturbing him. From the darkness echoed a faint laugh—a thin, ironic laugh, a laugh that thrilled Thady Shea with evil memories and swift apprehension. He seemed to recognize it as the laugh of Abel Dorales.

Before he could do more than lift his head and peer into the darkness, that darkness was suddenly split and rended by a red flash. The crack of a weapon lifted and lessened among the hills; as it died away, the baby cried out, whimpering. Across the face of Thady Shea flickered a look of dismay, of surprise, of utmost horror. Thady Shea took a step backward, as though something had lifted him off his balance, as though something unseen had impacted against him with terrific force. He staggered and lifted both hands to his head. Then his knees seemed to loosen, and he pitched downward, at the very brink of the gully.

From the stony ravine below came a heavy sound, as of a body pitching and dragging downward. It ceased, and there was abrupt silence. In that silence, the baby cried out, whimpering thinly.

Into the circle of light cast by the tiny fire came a man leading a pony. The man was Abel Dorales and he was smiling.

CHAPTER XV

MACKINTAVERS MAKES FRIENDS

MRS. CRUMP was grimly jubilant. She had just killed, not far from the shack which she inhabited, a rattler. It was a peculiarly deadly rattler, a big diamond-back, and its black-and-yellow body looked very beautiful lying out in the morning sunlight.

Mrs. Crump had killed that rattler most expertly; she had killed it with one snapping crack of a blacksnake whip. That one whip snap had coiled about the rattler's head and had neatly decapitated the reptile. Somewhere among the rocks that head lay naked and ugly, jaws wide agape, white fangs gleaming like needles.

Now, up on the long hogback, Mrs. Crump directed the work of getting out ore, Lewis and Gilbert working steadily under her orders. There was already a goodly heap of ore ready for hauling. Mrs. Crump was awaiting the arrival of Coravel Tio, whom she expected hourly; she had written Coravel Tio very explicitly, and was looking forward to making some money in the near future.

When Coravel Tio arrived, they would arrange about getting a light truck to haul the ore to railroad, and they would arrange about selling the ore. Coravel Tio would handle all such details. Actual production was well under way, and inside of another month Mrs. Crump hoped to have a good force of men working. Provided, of course, that the mine was not sold outright.

"Looks like he's a-coming." Gilbert swung out his hand toward the trail from No Agua. Shading her eyes, Mrs. Crump perceived a smudge of white dust. An automobile was approaching.

It was not Coravel Tio who came, however. It was Sandy Mackintavers, driven in a hired car from Magdalena.

Mehitabel Crump was stiff-necked and uncompromising. She stood in the door of her shack, storm in her eyes, and waited grimly. Outside, sprawled on a bench that ran the length of the shack, Lewis and Gilbert smoked and also waited, ready to act if called upon.

Sandy Mackintavers left his automobile and approached the shack, quick to note the arrangements for his reception. He came up to the doorway where Mrs. Crump awaited him. He removed his hat as he came, and mopped his brow; the sun was pitiless, streaming down with direct and scorching glare, absolute and insufferable. In another hour or two it would be much worse. Sandy Mackintavers held his hat in his left hand; he extended his right hand, square-fingered and strong, to Mrs. Crump.

"Madam, I have come here as a friend. Will you shake hands with me?"

"Not by a damn' sight!"

Mrs. Crump's eyes were snapping dangerously. Her retort did not seem to affect Mackintavers, however. His square-hewn features assumed an oddly hypocritical expression of patient resignation. His hand remained extended.

"I must explain. Your friend Shea has repaid the money—you understand?"

"Reckon I do. What about it?"

"We had quite a conversation, Mrs. Crump. That man is a wonder! Yes'm. Most remarkable! I never did see things so clear as he made me see 'em, aiblins yes. If I may say so, I feel ashamed of myself. I've done some unhandsome things; aiblins, now, I'll turn around. I'm right sorry for some things, Mrs. Crump. Will ye take my hand?"

Now, if there was anything which could shake the uncompromising hostility of Mrs. Crump, it was to hear her bitterest enemy praise Thady Shea. Aside from this, to hear Sandy Mackintavers express penitence for past sins, even to hear him admit that he had sinned, was an astounding thing. The incredibility of it was tremendous.

That mention of Thady Shea softened Mrs. Crump. She realized that Thady had made a great impression, had made so great an impression that here was Sandy Mackintavers, in the flesh, making apologies for past deeds!

"Well, Sandy," she returned, bluntly, "I will say that I think ye to be more or less of a skunk. Howsomever, I'll meet any man halfway—even you—when he talks that-a-way. I don't guess we'd ever be bosom friends, but I don't aim to be mean or ornery when a man's tryin' to be as white as his nature allows him. Here y'are."

She seized his hand and shook it vigorously. Mackintavers looked rather red about the face, as though her frank opinion of his character had bitten into him.

"Now, if you have time to be talkin' over a little matter o' business—"

"About this here location?" Mrs. Crump's eyes began to snap again.

"Yes."

"Gilbert! Lewis! Come on in here. Meet Sandy Mackintavers. They're members o' the company, Sandy. They got claims along the cañon, which same they turned in for stock. Stock ain't issued yet, but that's all right. Come on inside an' talk."

The lady was truculent and openly suspicious; the two men were narrow-eyed, hostile. Mackintavers seemed quite oblivious, and entered the shack. All four seated themselves. Mackintavers produced cigars. Mrs. Crump lighted her pipe and uttered a single emphatic word.

"Shoot!"

"You have a valuable mine here," said Mackintavers, without preamble. "I want to control it. I'm talking frank and laying my cards on the table, ma'am. First, let me give you folks an idea of the railroad situation."

He briefly described the prevalent car shortage, with the reasons therefore.

"You'll get no ore cars until the war's over, and maybe not then," he pursued. "But I have a standing contract that can't be broken, for so many cars a month—and I'm getting them. Ye see? Aiblins, now, that contract's worth something; set your own figure on it. For the rest, I'll buy stock at your own price, a controlling interest."

"Sandy, who'd ever trust you once ye got your nose into this thing?" Mrs. Crump laughed scornfully. "Not me!"

"Then don't trust me," returned Sandy, meekly, although the veins in his temples swelled into blue cords. "Don't trust me. Hire your own lawyers to draw up the matter, protect your interests fully. Give me charge of the actual mine, and then sit back an' draw down the coin from your interest; savvy? If I'm not able to make millions out o' this here mine, I'll quit! Ain't that frank talk? Ain't I human? I tell ye, when that man Shea came along and turned back that money, I learned something!"

"Where's Thady Shea now?" demanded Mrs. Crump.

"Went to St. Johns night before last, with Fred Ross and Bill Murray. Said he'd be here later, maybe. I like that man! Something about him kind o' draws you. Aiblins, he'd be grand in the legislature, now! Eh? Well, well, about this mine matter; as I say, use any means ye like. I don't blame you for not trusting me. But it's a good thing and I'll buy into it, savvy? Protect yourself, certainly. But why not let me buy into it? I have a bit of influence; aiblins, now, I'd be able to help production here an' there, and to furnish no end of money for the work."

The snap had gone out of Mrs. Crump's blue eyes. They were suddenly warm, kindly, unguarded. Thady Shea in the legislature! Why not? And Sandy was dead right. Everyone seemed to be drawn to Thady Shea.

There was some subsequent discussion to which Mackintavers himself put an end.

"Let it hang fire for a day or so, Mis' Crump. If ye don't mind, I'll hang around and look over the place and vicinity for my own self. Mebbe Shea will get back; the place is in his name, ain't it? Understood so."

"Yes," assented Mrs. Crump, unthinking. "And each of us owns a third interest, or at least, so it'll be arranged."

"And the other third?" Mackintavers looked swiftly at her. "I heard somethin' about a greaser up to Santy Fé making inquiries with Eastern firms about strontianite—that old curio dealer—Coravel Tio! He ain't the man, aiblins, now?"

"Yes. He'll be here to-day, I hope. All right, Sandy, let her hang over a day or so. I don't know but what we might consider it."

Mrs. Crump felt suddenly cold at that mention of Coravel Tio. How much had he discovered? He must have learned through Eastern connections that Coravel Tio had been making inquiries. Was this pose of honesty a blind, or not? What lay behind this visit? Had anything happened to Thady Shea?

She cursed herself furiously for having been beguiled even into listening to Sandy Mackintavers. Yet—why not? His proposal offered no loophole for trickery. Mrs. Crump would have preferred to sell the place entirely; but to retire in security and draw down fat dividends would be a very comfortable thing.

Late in the afternoon arrived Coravel Tio. He was mildly surprised to see Mackintavers. He was urbane, shy, suave, and professed great ignorance of everything. He readily listened to the plan of Mackintavers, and discussed it; but he reserved any opinion on the matter.

Mackintavers had sent his hired car back to Magdalena, and would bunk with Gilbert and Lewis for the night. Coravel Tio had driven his own car, which was fitted with a camping outfit. He made his own little camp down the cañon.

Late that evening, after all hands had retired to rest, Mrs. Crump picked her way down the rocky slope and joined Coravel Tio, who sat smoking beside his car.

"This here location is gettin' right crowded," she began, irritably, settling down and filling her corncob. "No chance even to speak a word no more! Well, what d'ye think o' this scheme? Don't it look to you like Sandy was tryin' to catch us off balance and topple us over?"

Coravel Tio showed his white teeth in a slow smile.

"Señora, let us go slowly. Let us go slowly. I really do not think that Mackintavers intends that we should consider his offer seriously. I think he is tricky about it. Well, he is about to come to a very high precipice, and is about to fall over that precipice; you see, I know something. I have information of which he is not aware. I have information which will prove very dangerous to him.

"About the mine. I have corresponded with the Williams Manufacturing Company of New Jersey, who are large manufacturers of chemical products. They will buy this location outright, should it prove up to the samples we sent. They are of the very highest standing and reputation; I have dealt with them for years. One of their men is due here any day; in fact, he is overdue. His name is James Z. Premble. He will be empowered to make full negotiations with us. Until he arrives, let us not worry about Mackintavers."

"Mebbe that's how come Sandy learned about your stake in the game; he knew you'd been correspondin' with somebody," and Mrs. Crump frowned. "My land! He's in with a heap o' them mining sharps, Coravel. They know all about each other."

Coravel Tio smiled gently. "Very likely, señora. However, this firm is entirely above suspicion. Now, we must find your friend Shea at once; that is imperative. The property is recorded in his name, you remember."

"Sandy knows that, too," said Mrs. Crump, her eyes troubled. "He knows too damned much, if you ask *me!*"

"Fear not, señora. He has been meddling with forbidden things, things which bring their own punishment. He has been meddling with things that I would not meddle with! By the way, I met a very interesting man the other day; one Thomas Twofork, an Indian from the Cochiti pueblo, recently returned from an Eastern college. You would enjoy meeting him. A very fine young man."

Mrs. Crump grunted. "I'd admire to know just what's laying back in your mind, Coravel Tio! Now, why the devil would I want to know any Injun buck like him? What's he to me?"

Coravel Tio laughed softly and puffed at his cigarette.

"Ah! I cannot say, señora. I am a curio dealer, no more. I know nothing at all about such things as these. But I know that Thomas Twofork is a very interesting man."

With the following morning Mrs. Crump took Mackintavers over the ground and the adjacent claims. Coravel Tio complained of the heat, and did not accompany them. Instead, he stood out in the sun, heedless of the heat, and watched Lewis and Gilbert at work. He talked with them at some length, and they seemed much interested in his discourse. By this time they knew a little more about Coravel Tio than they had known at their first meeting with him.

"What do you figger is goin' to happen, then?" demanded Lewis, when he had finished.

"I do not know." Coravel Tio shrugged his shoulders. "But it is well to know what might have to be done, eh? Ah, yes."

The morning wore on. Mrs. Crump retired to her own shack to cook luncheon, with much grumbling about the way the country was getting crowded up, and if many more folks came in she'd have to seek other quarters, and so on. Secretly, she was much pleased to exhibit her culinary skill, which was considerable.

At length she energetically hammered a pie pan, and the four men assembled. Gilbert was the last to come in from the mine over the flank of the hogback.

"Looks like some puncher is headed this way," he announced, eagerly. "Feller comin' on hossback, looks like he's headin' down from that big cañon north of here."

"My land!" ejaculated Mrs. Crump in dismay. "Wait till I get another plate set."

"No hurry," returned Gilbert. "I seen him top a rise four mile north. Ain't no rush, ma'am. He'll be quite a spell gettin' here. Lots o' bad land in between and no trail."

They sat down to the meal.

Outside, the sun was beating down in waves of heat. It was a pitiless, insufferable sun. Few things could stand that beating, merciless sun and still enjoy it. Out among the stones, what was left of the big diamond-back was withered and scorched. Some distance away, the head of the rattler lay among the rocks, dead jaws wide agape, white fangs gleaming like needles in the beating sunlight.

Inside the shack, the heat was intense; it filled the cañon as heat fills an oven, and here was no cool adobe walls to break its force. The heat had odd and curious effects upon the five people gathered there. It did not seem to touch Coravel Tio or the two miners in the least. Mackintavers it coarsened and reddened and thickened with pitiless breath. Mrs. Crump it softened; flushed and perspiring from cooking, she seemed to have become less harsh, more feminine, altogether transformed.

Suddenly, while they were eating, Coravel Tio looked up sharply and appeared to be listening. Then, one after another, the others glanced up, surprise in their eyes. The sharp and staccato pulse of an approaching automobile was to be heard. Another car!

Mrs. Crump led the exodus. Beside her own car and that of Coravel Tio, a third car was standing; a hired car from Magdalena, the same which had brought Mackintavers on the previous day. From this car alighted a man who carried a suitcase and bag, upon each of which were printed the letters J. Z. P. He was a man of citified aspect, and he approached the party clumped around the shack doorway with a stiff gaze and a businesslike air.

"I am looking for a lady by the name of Crump, Mrs. Crump," said he, setting down his suitcase and doffing his hat to the lady in question. "I presume that you are the lady named; if so you may be expecting me. My name is James Z. Premble."

Mrs. Crump recovered from her surprise and stepped forward.

"I'm her," she announced. "Glad to meet ye, Premble. Here, let me heft them grips inside the shack."

Gilbert, however, was ahead of her in the task. But James Z. Premble disregarded them both. He had come to a staring pause. Across his city-pale features swept an expression of amazement and gusty anger. His eyes were fastened upon Sandy

Mackintavers, and back at him was staring Mackintavers, wearing a look of consternation. Mr. Premble lifted one arm and shook a milk-white fist in air.

"You low-down hound!" he snapped at Sandy. "Didn't I warn you to keep away from me? What are you trying to—"

"Shut your fool mouth!" roared Mackintavers. "No need of airing things here."

"I'll say what I dashed please!" affirmed Premble, glaring. "I suppose you own this place, eh? I suppose you told some lying tale and these people swallowed it! Well, you can't shut me up. You can't gag *me!* You're about the worst swindler that ever kept out of State's prison, get that? You may be running this place, but you'll not run me."

"Hush up, pilgrim!" Mrs. Crump stepped in front of Premble and assumed charge of the situation. "Hush up! Sandy don't own this place, and he ain't runnin' nothin'. You a friend of his?"

"Friend? *Friend?*" Mr. Premble hoarsely gasped the word. "I wouldn't be his friend if he would give me a million dollars! I wouldn't be his friend if I was the last man and he was the last woman on earth! Why, that rogue played the worst low-down trick on me over in El Paso that—"

"Well, repress the sentiments," urged Mrs. Crump, calmly. "I guess we coincide with your feelin's, more or less, but at the present moment Sandy is a guest on this here prop'ty, which same prop'ty belongs to me, more or less. You're a guest likewise and I don't aim to have no ruction start between two o' my guests. I don't know you, Mr. Premble, and I don't know as I want to know ye, having a mean and rollin' eye like you have; but you're here on business and that goes as it lays. No war talk! Savvy?"

With a mighty effort Mr. Premble composed his features.

"Very well, madam, very well," he returned, stiffly. "You may depend upon it, there will be no more trouble—unless I meet this man the other side of your property line."

"You won't," said Mrs. Crump, grimly. "Come on in and set to dinner. Gilbert, you done? Then call that there driver to come up and have a bite, will ye? No words out'n you, neither, Sandy Mackintavers. Gents, come inside an' smoke up and entertain Mr. Premble. I'll get them 'tatoes het up in a mite."

First to enter the shack was James Z. Premble. He passed Mackintavers, standing at the door, and glared at him. Then, as he passed on into the shack, the features of Mr. Premble relaxed into the fleetest and most momentary shadow of a grin.

CHAPTER XVI

DORALES POSTS NOTICES

THE EXCITEMENT caused by the arrival of James Z. Premble caused everyone to forget the horseman who had been seen approaching from the north. And Mr. Premble, somewhat against his inmost desire, continued for a time to fill the centre of the picture.

The assemblage quite filled the shack—crowded it, in fact. Premble, the New Yorker, barely paused for introductions before diving into the food that Mrs. Crump set before him. Lewis sat and smoked in the lean-to, by the stove; Gilbert lounged beside the door. Mackintavers sat in the corner, chewing a cigar. Coravel Tio was rolling a cigarette with great care, and sighed a little as he licked it; leaning forward, he scratched a match upon the floor, and took advantage of a pause in the conversation to address James Z. Premble.

"An odd name, señor," he said, softly. "A very odd name! I have never met any one whose initial was that of Z. May I ask what name it stands for, señor?"

Mr. Premble looked at his questioner, and in his shrewd eyes there showed a swift and sudden hesitation; but Coravel Tio was lighting his cigarette with much absorption.

"Zacariah," responded the New Yorker. "I don't like the name, myself. Never use it."

"Ah, yes! Now that I remember, I have met others—there is a name Zebulon, I think, eh? Yes, Zebulon. So you are the gentleman of whom your firm wrote me, eh? I am glad to meet you, señor, very glad. You have letters and so forth? You see, I am part owner of this property, señor, and while I do not doubt you in the least, I desire to make quite sure of things before talking business."

Laying down his knife and fork, Premble once again inspected Coravel Tio, who was now looking directly at him. Something in those gentle, mournful black eyes seemed to cause the city man uneasiness and disquiet. He reached into his pocket, nodding.

"Eh? Sure, I have plenty of papers that will establish my identity and prove my authority to deal with you. A little bit hasty, aren't you? No trouble, though. Glad to have you assure yourself—"

He produced a sheaf of papers and passed them intact, as though entirely certain of their contents, to Mrs. Crump. That lady, her keen blue eyes suddenly perplexed and watchful, handed on the papers to Coravel Tio. The latter, in silence, began to unfold and look at them, one after another. Premble continued his meal, and fell to talking with the others.

Presently Coravel Tio came to the end of his cigarette. He rose and tossed the butt through the open doorway, where Gilbert was lounging. His eyes snapped a message to those of Gilbert; in turn, Gilbert made a slight motion. Lewis rose and shoved aside the curtain from the window, as though desiring more air, and then stood watching.

Coravel Tio returned to his stool. At another pause in the conversation, he tapped the refolded documents on his knee.

"These are all correct, Mr. Premble," he said, gently. "Do you know—ah, there is something that puzzles me! Now, when I had the pleasure of meeting you in Las Vegas last month, your name was different; it was Zebulon and not Zacariah. And you looked different, señor. Then, if I remember rightly, you wore a moustache, and your eyes were another colour, and you had a stronger chin than you have at present."

A sudden tense silence had come upon the room. James Z. Premble looked very red, then his features paled again. Imperceptibly, his right hand fluttered toward his left armpit.

"Don't do it!" said Lewis, from the window, and Mr. Premble gazed into the muzzle of a revolver. And: "Go slow!" said Gilbert, from the doorway, carelessly fondling another revolver. Mr. James Z. Premble set both hands upon the table in front of him.

The chauffeur, seeing the general trend of events, quietly slid from his stool and vanished beneath the table. Mrs. Crump sat motionless, looking from one person to another. Sandy Mackintavers swallowed hard and made as if to rise, but Lewis shifted eyes and weapon slightly, and Sandy changed his mind about moving.

"I was afraid of something like this." The voice of Coravel Tio was gently apologetic. "You see, the real James Zebulon Premble always keeps his engagements to the minute—unless something has happened to him. He is now two days overdue here. Of course, it would be possible for another man to waylay him and to obtain his papers; it would be quite possible for that other man to come here under the name of Premble, and to carry out a slight business transaction."

"Smooth guy, aren't you?" sneered Premble. "You'll have a hell of a time proving anything on me!"

"My dear señor, I don't want to prove anything on you!" said Coravel Tio in pained surprise. "No, no, far from it! But I suspect that a certain firm by the name of the Williams Manufacturing Company, a firm that is very jealous of its reputation, might like to know that you are in its employ. Si! Of course, you'll not reveal to us for whom you are working?"

"I've nothing to say," sullenly returned Premble. He looked much perturbed.

"Very well. Gilbert, take the gun from the señor's left armpit and lead him to his automobile. Tie him in his automobile and allow him to repose in peaceful meditation. That is all. Young man, kindly come from beneath the table and resume your meal!"

The chauffeur, looking sheepish, crawled into view again. Gilbert fulfilled the orders that had been given him, and departed with Mr. Premble.

Sandy Mackintavers, although trying to appear impassive and unconcerned, signally failed in his endeavour. He was completely astounded, swept off his feet, by the falling of Coravel Tio's mask. He was suddenly aware of the fact that in Coravel Tio he had a damnably clever antagonist.

Now, too late, Sandy began to suspect a thousand things that did not appear on the surface. Conjectures flitted through his brain. Suspicion that the hand of Coravel Tio was a very powerful hand, and that this hand was set against him, deepened into hard certainty. Yet—not even Coravel Tio could know the truth! No one could know that Mackintavers and the false Premble were friends, were working in concert! There was yet hope.

"Aiblins, now, there's no tellin' about these mining sharks!" observed Sandy in righteous accents. "I've had experiences of my own in that line, aye! But if you're willing to talk over the proposition we discussed last night—"

Coravel Tio looked at him. Coravel Tio laughed gently, softly, very acridly.

"My dear señor!" he said. "You knew about the real Premble and his business here. Your friend met the real Premble and did his work very well. You planned things nicely. You came and made us your proposition, knowing that we would refuse it, knowing that we would be assured that you and Premble were

at enmity; knowing that we would sell out to Señor Premble—
eh? And Premble would buy the mine for you. Ah, yes!

"It was very cleverly planned, and very well executed. But
now, señor, you had better go and sit beside your friend, and be
driven back to town with him. There I think that you will receive
some interesting information. I would like to tell you about it
myself, but—"

At this point Mrs. Crump came to her feet. She understood
the whole trick at last, she understood the deep cunning of
Mackintavers, and she was white with fury.

"Coravel Tio, this skunk sure makes me blush to see him!
Now, I aim to give him a right good hidin', which same he
deserves plenty. Get outside, ye coyote—hustle!"

From the wall Mrs. Crump seized her trusty blacksnake.
Thoroughly alarmed, Mackintavers attempted no protests but
backed through the doorway. Before the lady, however, uprose
Coravel Tio, and his hand restrained her from pursuit.

"No," he said, softly, looking into her eyes. "I have reasons,
señora; good reasons."

Mrs. Crump flushed, then paled again. Restraint came hard
to her.

"I aim to punish him," she rasped.

"That is already arranged." Coravel Tio smiled at her. "That
has been arranged—by the gods of the San Marcos. You will,
please, leave everything in my hands, señora. Everything! I wish
to handle everything here to-day. Everything!"

Mrs. Crump stared at him, puzzled. Then she tossed away
the whip.

"All right," she assented, sullenly, angrily. "I won't say another
damned word."

By this time, Mackintavers was somewhere outside. Lewis
still stood by the window. Gilbert was presumably down at the
automobiles with his prisoner.

But now the voice of Gilbert came to them. It was lifted in
a shout of surprise, a shout of aggrieved anger and amazement.

"Hey! Hey, you feller! What the hell you doin' there? Hey, Mis' Crump! Hustle out here!"

Those in the shack hastened outside—all except the chauffeur. Scenting further trouble, that gentleman grabbed his plate and again retired beneath the table, to finish his meal in security.

As Mrs. Crump, standing out in the sunlight, surveyed the situation, she became aware that the previously discerned horseback rider had arrived. He had evidently ridden right over the long flank of the hogback, past the mine workings, into the cañon. Fifty yards up the cañon, fifty yards above the two shacks, lay a horse that was weary unto death, a horse that had been ridden hard and furiously, without mercy.

Not far from the horse was something white. This was a piece of new, white paper that had been fastened to Mrs. Crump's original location notice.

Down below the shacks, between them and the automobiles, was another scrap of white; another piece of white paper fastened over another location notice. Standing only a few yards from the shack, and hurriedly talking to Mackintavers, stood the rider who had just arrived. The man was Abel Dorales. He had just put up those two notices, and he paid no attention whatever to the threatening approach of Gilbert.

"Dorales!" gasped Mrs. Crump, and whirled. "Lewis! Here! Gi'me that gun!"

"Stop!" Coravel Tio grasped her arm. "Stop, señora! Force does nothing. Leave things in my hands, *si servase!* Lewis, go and tell Gilbert to be quiet—*pronto!*"

The potently gentle voice of Coravel Tio held firm command. He was obeyed. Gilbert stood motionless, scowling; Mrs. Crump stayed her hand.

Mackintavers walked quickly toward Mrs. Crump and Coravel Tio; eagerness shone in his eyes, and exultation. Behind him strode Abel Dorales, fixedly regarding Mrs. Crump. The half-breed's features were thinly cruel; his nostrils quivered slightly; a shadowy smile curved his lips into sneering lines.

Gilbert turned and walked toward the new notice posted by Dorales.

"Just got some news," said Mackintavers, jerkily. "Abel is goin' to stay and tell ye bout it. I don't s'pose ye got any objection if I light out for Magdalena, aiblins, now?"

Coravel Tio was rolling a cigarette, quite unconcernedly. He flashed Sandy a smile.

"Object? Why should we object, señor? By all means, go! And take your friend with you, your friend whose name is Zacariah and not Zebulon. *Vaya con Dios, señor!*"

Mackintavers was plainly in haste to be off. He called to the chauffeur, who came from the shack and joined him. Together the two walked rapidly toward the car wherein was reposing the bogus James Z. Premble.

"Y' ain't goin' to let them varmints go?" Mrs. Crump surveyed Coravel Tio with pleading indignation. "After them tryin'—"

Gracefully, Coravel Tio waved his cigarette. "Si, *señora!* Let them go. Let them both go. There are larger things, much larger things, awaiting us."

"But that feller Premble!"

"Let them both go, señora. We have larger things ahead."

Mrs. Crump sniffed in uncomprehending disgust; but she gave tacit assent.

The engine of the car began to whir; the whir became a roaring hum, then a deep vibrant thrumming that lifted through the cañon. The car, with its three men, moved away and leaped into speed.

"Hey!" The voice of Gilbert, who had been reading the new location notice, drifted up to them. "Hey! This guy is jumpin' our claim! He's posted notices in the name o' Mackintavers. What the hell!"

"Come up here, Gilbert," said Coravel Tio, "and keep quiet. We are to hear some news. Ah, Señor Dorales, have you lunched? We are glad to welcome you."

Dorales did not reply. He did not move, but upon his lips lingered that thin, shadowy smile that was like the stamp of a cruel jeer. Gilbert heavily came up and rejoined the others.

They stood there at the doorway of the shack—Mrs. Crump, Coravel Tio, Gilbert, and Lewis. Facing them stood Abel Dorales; he seemed to be waiting until the automobile should have gotten away beyond pursuit. Already it was a dot, lessening amid a trail of dust. In the bearing of Abel Dorales was a commanding air, a deep significance, a sneering sense of power. He was in no hurry to explain.

The sun beat down in vertical, sickening waves; the heat was suffocating, insufferable. It filled the cañon like an oven. To the left lay the spent horse, panting, loose-tongued, exhausted, unable even to reach the trickle of water below. No other thing moved within sight. Behind and above rose the long hogback that formed the north wall of the cañon. It shut out from view all that lay beyond, all that lay over toward the mountains and the larger cañon that drew out from the mountains to the north.

The ground seemed to radiate heat in shimmering waves. To one side lay the dry and withered body of the rattler Mrs. Crump had killed—what was left by the preying tiny things of the earth. Somewhere among the rocks lay that reptilian head, what was left of it. Inconspicuous it was, unseen, dead jaws agape and long fangs glimmering like needles in the hot, sickening sunlight.

"Yes," said Abel Dorales at last. "Yes. I have some news for you."

He ignored that offer of luncheon. He ignored the lowering, menacing looks of Lewis and Gilbert. He ignored the suave Coravel Tio. He fixedly regarded Mrs. Crump, hatred flaming in his dark eyes and quivering at his nostrils. He had hated her from the depths of his soul ever since that day he had jumped her claim over in the Mogollons, that day when she had shot him down like a dog.

There was nothing melodramatic in his bearing. He was grimed with dust and dirt. He was perspiring profusely; his lined and evil face was streaming with sweat against its sleek bronze. He had ridden hard, and he was tired.

Suddenly he shifted his gaze and looked around, to right and left, at the shimmering and empty cañon. He looked at the farther hill on the other side. He looked up at the long hogback which closed in those five persons, shutting out all the rest of the world like a vast door of rock. He looked up toward the mountain peaks that showed above the head of the cañon. Some inward sense seemed to whisper to him a warning against eavesdroppers; but all the visible world was glowing with insufferable heat, and was deserted. His eyes gleamed with satisfaction.

"What for ye postin' notices on my lands?" demanded Mrs. Crump. "Huh? How come ye sent Mackintavers off to file the claims at the recordin' office, huh? What ye expect to gain by all that fool play, huh? Speak up, ye mangy dog!"

Abel Dorales looked at her, and smiled thinly. "One moment," he said.

Turning, Abel Dorales strode up the cañon to where lay his exhausted horse. The poor brute made a painful struggle as if to rise; forefeet, neck, and shoulders heaved convulsively, then collapsed again. Abel Dorales kicked the horse with contempt. From the saddle he took a battered little yellow suitcase which had been tied there and he started back.

At a word from Coravel Tio, the others moved into the slender shadow cast by the north side of the shack, the side that faced uphill to the hogback. There Abel Dorales rejoined them. There he set the battered little suitcase on the ground.

"I should have given this to Sandy," he said, "but I forgot it. Now, Mrs. Crump, your friend Shea stole this from the ranch of Mackintavers. Here is what he stole."

With a swift movement he opened the suitcase and dumped out the seven stone gods. They strewed the ground in grotesque attitudes. One fell upright, grinning stonily as if delighted by the feat. Dorales tossed the little suitcase away.

"Ah, yes!" It was Coravel Tio who spoke, unexpectedly. He spoke as though in recognition. "The gods of the San Marcos! But you are wrong, señor. Our friend Shea did not steal these things. They were stolen by a Navaho, a buck who was hired to steal them because he knew the ranch house of Mackintavers very well. He was hired by Thomas Twofork, who comes from the Cochiti pueblo. These gods were the gods of the San Marcos, you understand, and they were the gods of Thomas Twofork's fathers. That Navaho buck was killed in an accident. How Señor Shea obtained these gods, I do not know."

Dorales laughed.

"It doesn't matter particularly now. Anyway, we'll concede that Shea didn't steal them, eh? All right. Sandy wanted these gods back, so I fetched them along. In my hurry to get this property located, I forgot to give them—"

"Where's Thady Shea?" cried out Mrs. Crump, suddenly. "Where is he?"

Abel Dorales looked at her, his lips curving in cruel enjoyment.

"Dead. This location was in his name. I believe that he is without heirs; since he is dead, I believe that his location reverts to the government. Whoever is first to file upon it, gets it. You see? The notices have been posted. Sandy has gone to file the location—now do you understand?"

"Liar!" Mrs. Crump flung the word at him in blind, gasping incredulity. "He ain't dead! Thady Shea ain't dead!"

"Oh, you need not blame me!" said Dorales, and laughed again. "I followed him, yes; but I came too late. I found him in a cañon over on the divide—Beaver Cañon."

"There was a Mexican refugee camped there with his family; a sheep-herder. Shea had come and had drunk mescal. He had become drunk, beastly drunk. I am not certain of what took place, because unfortunately I arrived too late—but the woman was dead, and Shea had fallen over the edge of a gully, breaking his neck. He had been shot, also. I think the woman must have shot him—first."

Under the lash of these slow words, delivered with a frightful appearance of truth, Mrs. Crump had gone quite livid. A hoarse, inarticulate growl came from her throat. The mortal pallor of a fury beyond all control came upon her; she trembled with sheer passion.

Then she started forward—but the hand of Coravel Tio gripped into her wrist.

CHAPTER XVII

DORALES RUNS AWAY

"LOOK!" SAID the soft voice of Coravel Tio. "Look up at the skyline!" Mrs. Crump tore herself free from that restraining hand—but she looked. She looked up, beyond Abel Dorales, above Abel Dorales, at the line of the hogback that cleaved across the hot blue sky. She stood thus, looking, wonder upon her.

There, clear-cut and sharp against the quivering blue sky, appeared three figures. They were the figures of a horse and two men; one of the men carried a bundle in his arms. This last figure sank again from sight almost instantly, as did that of the horse. The figure of the other man came down the steep slope, came down swiftly and eagerly.

Abel Dorales saw Mrs. Crump look upward. He saw the others follow her gaze, saw the startled and wondering surmise that filled their eyes. He turned, catlike, and looked. He stared at that tall figure, whose clothes were torn and dishevelled, whose forehead was streaked by the raw, red brand of a hot bullet. He stared at that figure, which was coming down the hillside rapidly toward him.

"*Dios!*" he whispered, throatily. "*Jesus Maria!*"

He crossed himself; the gesture was made in terrible, spasmodic haste. His arms flung out wide, palms backward as though in search of some support. He took a retreating step, and another, as that tall figure strode down at him; he backed against a bowlder and stood thus, staring. His brown face became ghastly pale, his mouth opened in slavering horror.

In his madness there was reason. He had come here quickly, very quickly, after shooting Thady Shea and seeing him topple into that gully; he knew that no other man could walk here and arrive so soon after he had arrived himself. He knew that this tall figure with the raw, red brand across the brow could be no living man.

"*Que quiere?*" he cried, huskily, with a great effort forcing his vocal chords to do their work. "*Que quiere?* What do you want, hell dweller?"

Mrs. Crump, who did not believe in ghosts, and who was not easily shaken off her balance, satisfied herself that it was really Thady Shea who approached. Then she slipped to the doorway of the shack and picked up the blacksnake whip which she had tossed away. She stood at the corner of the shack, waiting, watching Abel Dorales, her lips grimly clenched into a thin line. She was quite content to let Thady Shea settle his own score with the man.

Thady came forward, wordless, his gaze fastened upon Dorales, deep anger gleaming in those intensely black eyes. Abel Dorales, ashen white, edged around the side of the bowlder. His hand drifted to his pocket; it flashed up again with a revolver.

But as Abel Dorales swung down that revolver, as he drew down on Thady Shea for a desperate ghost-quelling shot, something snaked out through the air—something that seemed to leap from the expert arm of Mehitabel Crump. It curled about the wrist of Abel Dorales, it curled and clung with vicious snap about his hand and fingers; as the head of a rattlesnake is snapped and tugged from his body with one whipcrack, so the revolver was torn from the hand of Dorales and sent flying out upon the stones.

Thady Shea flung himself upon Dorales.

As has been previously seen, Thady Shea knew nothing about the science and art of fighting. His was a blind, primitive, untutored lust for vengeance. He had heard that resonant voice telling the story of his death; he had heard, lifting to him above the crest of the hogback, that false tale designed to blacken his memory, and now he plunged headlong at Abel Dorales, angered as he had never been angered in his life.

Stricken and all unstrung by what he had taken to be an apparition, Abel Dorales tried to stumble away, cowering. But in a moment the furious, clumsy blows of Thady Shea proved that here was real flesh and blood; Shea landed one smash that all but stove in the ribs of his enemy. In his arms was terrific strength, had he but known how to use it. Perhaps it was as well that the knowledge was lacking, else Dorales had died very brutally and quickly.

Still retreating, Dorales gathered himself together and faced the storm. He saw that this was no ghost, but a man of flesh and blood—a man very weary, very terrible, a man whose consuming anger swept away all sense of bodily hurt and weariness. Dorales blocked the furious blows, then, most incautiously, allowed Thady Shea to clinch.

That was near to being the death of Dorales, for now the terrific strength of Thady Shea poured forth like a flood. The two men locked, reeled back and forth, went plunging down to the stones. They rolled down the hillside; they fought with utter madness—yet ever the steel arms were tightening about the body of Dorales, ever the ribs of Dorales were cracking and giving inward.

In that primitive and sickening struggle, neither man saw or gave heed to anything else than the face of his foe. Neither man observed that, as they upheaved and rolled again, they had come upon something that gleamed like needles in the sunlight; something wide and gaping that lay there unseen and inconspicuous among the stones.

Desperate, feeling the very life wrenching out of him, Abel Dorales flung loose one arm and attempted to clutch a stone, wherewith to batter at the deadly face above him. The two men writhed again, heaved upward, fell heavily in a twisted mass. Something thin and piercing, something that gleamed like white needles in the sunlight, ripped the skin of Dorales' outflung arm. Upon that arm fell all the plunging weight of Thady Shea, grinding it down upon the stones, grinding with it the gaping jaws of that rattler's head, grinding arm and jaws until the skin, from wrist to elbow, was burst and ripped asunder as cloth is ripped before a knife.

The pain of this unseen, blind hurt fired Dorales into frantic efforts. He flung Shea backward; he hammered in one blow and another, rocking back Shea's head and blinding him. Dorales gained his feet once more, writhing free, panting. He was freed of Shea's grip. His arm was dripping blood. Dorales looked down at Thady Shea, who was weakly rising to throw himself forward anew—then Abel Dorales turned. He turned and ran, bounding and sliding to the cañon floor in great leaps, running wildly and blindly past the two automobiles, running from the vengeance of the man whom he had tried to murder, the man who now seemed to be more than man. But Thady Shea did not pursue, for now weakness and dizziness had come upon him, and after two steps Shea fell forward.

From the doorway of the shack came a sharp report; a fleck of dust lifted, slightly to one side of the running figure of Dorales. There came a second report, and a fleck of dust lifted from between the running feet of Dorales. Mrs. Crump was throwing down for the third and final shot when Coravel Tio wrenched her arm aside.

"For the love of Heaven, stop!" cried Coravel Tio. "No murder, señora! Go and look after Shea—quick!"

He tore the revolver away from her; then he watched Abel Dorales until the half-breed turned a bend in the cañon and was lost to sight.

Gilbert and Lewis had run to lift Thady Shea, and Mrs. Crump joined them. Tears shone upon her cheeks as Thady Shea came to his feet and faintly smiled at her. His lips moved, and a panting whisper reached her ears.

"The baby—look after—her! I—knew—you wouldn't mind—"

"Carry him into the shack, ye galoots!" snapped Mrs. Crump, crisply, one hand dabbing the tears from her eyes. "Can't you see his mind's wanderin'? Hurry up, now!"

Despite Shea's protest, they obeyed her mandate. She followed them as far as the shack doorway, then paused. Another man had come down from the hogback, had suddenly appeared from nowhere, and was talking with Coravel Tio; another man, tall and swarthy of face, behind whom followed a saddled pony. The pony was very weary.

It was not the man at whom Mrs. Crump looked, however. It was the bundle in his arms which drew her startled attention—that bundle was unmistakably a baby! She realized that Thady Shea had not been wandering in his mind after all. It was a baby, a little brown baby who was cooing and laughing in the face of Coravel Tio.

Hastily, Mrs. Crump stepped forward, Coravel Tio turned to meet her.

"Señora, this is my friend Thomas Twofork, of whom I told you. He has been following those gods of the San Marcos, and now he has found them."

Coravel Tio gestured toward the earth, where lay the seven stone gods sprawled in grotesque attitudes, one alone being upright, grinning stonily. But Mrs. Crump paid no heed to him or to the smiling Thomas Twofork. From the latter's infolding arms she seized the baby with a sudden and fierce gesture.

"Where'd ye get it? Where'd Thady Shea get it?" she demanded, sharply.

Thomas Twofork, standing there in the sunlight, told his story, while Mrs. Crump fondled the baby with admiration and kindliness growing in her keen blue eyes.

Thomas Twofork had located that battered yellow suitcase at the Hotel Aragon, had seen Thady Shea depart with it—and had found the fan belt on his own car broken. While repairing it, he had become aware that Dorales was also on the trail of Shea. Dorales had started westward, and after him, Twofork.

Dorales had not gone on to St. Johns, but had followed the tracks of Murray's car when it turned off on the trail to Old Fort Tularosa and Aragon. He had met Murray's car returning without Thady Shea, and had hastened on into Aragon; by the time he discovered that Shea had not been here, and had exchanged his car for a horse, much time was lost.

Dorales had gone back along the trail, had picked up Shea's track at daybreak, and had followed; after Dorales had gone Thomas Twofork, patiently unhurrying. Both men had met the ranger returning to town with the murderer, Garcia, and had learned Shea's route.

When Dorales had fired that shot in the night, Twofork had been waiting, had seen the act too late to prevent it. Dorales had at once taken the yellow suitcase, pushing forward without delay. Thomas Twofork had found Thady Shea in the gully, creased by the bullet, but unwounded, battered by the fall but sound of wind and limb. With Shea in the saddle, holding the baby, Thomas Twofork had followed the trail of Dorales quickly and unerringly.

The remainder was briefly told. Knowing that the hogback hid all the country beyond the view of those in the cañon, Thady Shea had waited until Dorales had ridden down into the cañon, then had come on with Thomas Twofork. Unseen, the two men had arrived, had waited; at the right moment, Thady Shea had made his appearance. As Thomas Twofork told it, the whole story was very simple, all very prosaic. But to those who had waited by the shack in the cañon, it had not been simple or prosaic. It had been very tragic and very terrible.

"So work the gods!" Coravel Tio tossed away his cigarette. "Thomas Twofork, here are the gods of your fathers; they are yours to take back to Cochiti. They have brought disaster upon Mackintavers and Dorales; they have brought us good blessings. And presently will come the real Premble, señora, to buy this mine of ours."

"What was that ye threatened Sandy about?" demanded Mrs. Crump, looking up from the baby for the first time. "That information ye mentioned?"

"Oh, that!" Coravel Tio laughed gently. "The grand jury is sitting at Santa Fé. I arranged a few things; a few affidavits, chief among them that of Señor Cota, one of our native legislators. I am confident that by this time Sandy Mackintavers has been indicted for bribery and other things. When he reaches Magdalena, he will find officers waiting for him. That is all. He paid too much attention to the gods of the San Marcos, and not enough attention to business. Ah, yes! Now, I am very curious to find what made so much blood upon the arm of Abel Dorales. I wonder, now!"

He beckoned to Thomas Twofork. The two men walked away, their eyes intent upon the stony ground of the hillside.

Mrs. Crump went into the cabin, bearing the baby. Somewhat to her surprise, she found Thady Shea sitting at the table, enjoying a hearty meal by the aid of Gilbert and Lewis.

"My land, Thady. I thought ye was plumb laid out. So ye've come back at last, huh? Well, set steady a while till I get some water on the stove—got to fix this here baby up a bit. Pore little critter! Don't know when I've seen a baby chortle like this here one."

Presently she had disposed the baby upon her own bunk, and found that the two men had gone. She was alone in the shack with Thady Shea and the baby. She went to the table and extended her hand.

"Thady," she said, her blue eyes moist, "have—have ye forgiven me that blow?"

He stood awkwardly, gripping her hand, a glow spreading over his face as he read the message in her eyes. Seldom had he seen her eyes look so tender, so womanly.

"What blow? I don't—oh! Why, I had really forgotten it."

"I ain't. It's sore mem'ry," said Mrs. Crump, bluntly. "Thady, when that varmint told that yarn about you bein' dead and so on, I was fixin' to kill him—yes, I was! In another minute I'd ha' done it, too. And now," suddenly her voice became crisp and harsh, defiantly harsh, "what ye mean bringin' that baby around here? D'you reckon I got time and room to take care o' babies?"

A look of pained astonishment came to the man's eye.

"Why—why, I intended to take care of that baby myself! She seemed to like me—"

"Who wouldn't, ye blunderin' big heart of a man!" she returned, softly. "Yes, I reckon that baby is goin' to stay right here, Thady Shea. I just wanted to see the idea in your mind, and now I reckon I know. Yes, sir! I reckon I know."

"You don't know—at least not all of it." Thady Shea was smiling now, smiling down into her eyes. "That baby is dependent on me; I'm going to make her happy! And she isn't all, either. I'm an old man and pretty useless, but—but I found a big purpose that has drawn me back here—and—and I want to tell you—"

Out upon the stony hillside, out in the blinding white sunlight, Coravel Tio and Thomas Twofork were standing together. In his hand the Indian held something—something fragmentary and crushed, something that glittered like broken needles in the sunlight.

"It was the head of a rattlesnake," said Thomas Twofork, meditatively, "and not long dead. You see? The fangs caught in his arm. The two men fell and ground into the stones the arm and fang together; the fangs were ripped along his arm—"

"Ah, yes! It is very wonderful." Coravel Tio began to roll a cigarette. He gazed down the cañon where the running figure of Abel Dorales had disappeared, and speculation filled his dreamy dark eyes.

"Was there any poison in the fangs? Very likely, Thomas Twofork. Perhaps it had been there in the moment of death; beyond doubt, it had been there. Was it dried up, too dried up to take effect? Well, we do not know. Soon, in a day or two, we shall know. One thing I do know, however—I know that *I* would never meddle with the gods of the San Marcos. Eh?"

Thomas Twofork was a college graduate, but he was first an Indian. To this last word of his companion he nodded solemn affirmation. The two men turned and started toward the shack; but a few yards from the doorway, they halted and glanced at each other. From the building had come a sudden low sound of a woman softly sobbing. Into the eyes of Thomas Twofork leaped a mute question. Coravel Tio answered with a gesture, and the two men changed their course and came to a halt near the automobiles.

"Well?" asked the Indian a moment later. "Why does she cry, Coravel Tio? Has that man Shea harmed her?"

Coravel Tio struck a match, lighted his cigarette, broke the match in two, and gracefully tossed away the fragments.

"No, he has not harmed her," he said, gently. "Yet she is sobbing; so, perhaps, is he. You do not understand these things, Thomas Twofork, but I am a philosopher. I understand everything! I have expected to hear the señora sob, thus, for some time past. Now it has happened. All is well."

"Eh?" The Indian scrutinized him in perplexity. "But what does it mean?"

"It means," and Coravel Tio smiled, "that the señora is very happy! She has found both a husband and a child. *Adios!*"

ABOUT THE AUTHOR

H. BEDFORD-JONES is a Canadian by birth, but not by profession, having removed to the United States at the age of one year. For over twenty years he has been more or less profitably engaged in writing and traveling. As he has seldom resided in one place longer than a year or so and is a person of retiring habits, he is somewhat a man of mystery; more than once he has suffered from unscrupulous gentlemen who impersonated him—one of whom murdered a wife and was subsequently shot by the police, luckily after losing his alias.

The real Bedford-Jones is an elderly man, whose gray hair and precise attire give him rather the appearance of a retired foreign diplomat. His hobby is stamp collecting, and his collection of Japan is said to be one of the finest in existence. At present writing he is en route to Morocco, and when this appears in print he will probably be somewhere on the Mojave Desert in company with Erle Stanley Gardner.

Questioned as to the main facts in his life, he declared there was only one main fact, but it was not for publication; that his life had been uneventful except for numerous financial losses, and that his only adventures lay in evading adventurers. In his younger years he was something of an athlete, but the encroachments of age preclude any active pursuits except that of motoring. He is usually to be found poring over his stamps, working at his typewriter, or laboring in his California rose garden, which is one of the sights of Cathedral Cañon, near Palm Springs.